T0152350

We Three

Jean Echenoz

WE THREE

Translated from the French by Jesse Anderson

DALKEY ARCHIVE PRESS

Despite its mission to support French literature in translation, and in particular to support the cause and well-being of translators, CNL (Centre national du livre) would not provide support for the translator of this book, and this at a time when there has been a substantial decrease in the number of books being translated into English. Dalkey Archive urges CNL to return to its mission of aiding translators.

Originally published in French as *Nous trois* by Minuit in 1992.

Library of Congress Cataloging-in-Publication Data
Names: Echenoz, Jean, author. | Anderson, Jesse, 1987- translator.
Title: We three / Jean Echenoz ; translated by Jesse Anderson.
Other titles: Nous trois. English
Description: Victoria, TX : Dalkey Archive Press, 2017.
Identifiers: LCCN 2016031190 | ISBN 9781628971705 (pbk. : alk. paper)
Subjects: LCSH: Man-woman relationships--Fiction. | Satirical literature.
Classification: LCC PQ2665.C5 N6813 2017 | DDC 843/.914--dc23
LC record available at https://lccn.loc.gov/2016031190

Partially funded by the Illinois Arts Council, a state agency.

www.dalkeyarchive.com
Victoria, TX / McLean, IL / Dublin

Cover: Art by Eric Longfellow

Dalkey Archive Press publications are, in part, made possible through the support of the University of Houston-Victoria and its programs in creative writing, publishing, and translation.

Printed on permanent/durable acid-free paper

1

I KNOW THE SKY QUITE WELL; the two of us have a long history together. All its shades of umber, lime, flesh, and saffron, I know. Sitting in my chair, out on the terrace, it has all my attention. It's noon. The sky is white. I've got all the time in the world.

No big plans for me on this lazy Monday, just two simple objectives to lightly fill in the evening: Max's private viewing at Pontarlier's, boulevard des Italiens, then Blondel's presentation at the agency's auditorium. I get up to go change: I search for and immediately find, among my hundred or so dress shirts, the perfect accompaniment for my plan. As usual, Titov is asleep in his corner.

At the end of the afternoon I duly called a taxi, the sky was as white as a sheet above boulevard des Italiens; Max was busy at the back of the gallery with a Japanese man. Pontarlier came toward me sweating and smiling beneath his scattered mustache—I trim mine more strictly—my blue eyes reflecting off his domed forehead. Have you seen yourself? he asked me while extracting a small hand from his pocket, soft and moist, which he then poured into my own—it was immediately drenched. His other hand held out a drink; I declined. His brittle teeth, disproportionately large and extremely flat, were almost transparent—in the back, some were even missing. Not yet, I responded. Go see yourself, said the gallery owner, go have a look at yourself.

I headed toward my smiling image: immaculate uniform in

front of a sky-blue background, my helmet beneath my arm, my identification badge over my right pectoral. The face on display there was from my first time working for the Americans: in reality I was smiling less in the photo, taken at Daytona, which Max had used for the portrait; afterward, I had to pose three or four times in his studio just so he could redo the smile. I briefly admired myself then made a tour of the gallery, dividing my attention between the other portraits and the other guests— none of the former resembled the latter, it seemed I was the only model in attendance. I lingered around a bit, threw a last glance toward the back of the gallery, things seemed heated between Max and the Japanese. Pontarlier had also gotten involved. I started toward the door.

Blondel was already partway through his speech when I entered the auditorium. Twenty people were there to watch his presentation, an annual report on the agency's activities. I easily found a place near the back of the room, not far from Bégonhès. The speaker had just gone over the original functions, mostly maritime, of our observation satellites—monitoring of solo sailors, excursionist albatrosses, and drifting icebergs—then described their current responsibilities—detection of flooding rivers, leaking nuclear power plants, and burning forests—before specifying their future roles: widespread military surveillance, that went without saying, but also remote control of oil pipeline gates, from the far ends of Arabia to the far ends of Alaska, along with management of railway networks and regulation of semitruck fleets. We'll be able to collect, prophesied Blondel, at any moment, any piece of information we want from any truck on earth—speed and oil level, temperature of refrigerated trailers, even the frequency of the car radio.

I already knew all this and so barely listened. I'd passed by simply to say hello. While waiting for Blondel to finish up, I considered without much interest the auditorium's decoration, tapestries to the sides and a big golden logo of the agency above the stage, toward the back. The twenty people present—rocket scientists, journalists, behaviorists, relatives and in-laws, the same two cross-legged girls who are always with the guy from the ministry—weren't paying much more attention to the presentation than I was. People spoke among themselves. Bégonhès, close by, flipped through the pages of a new avionics reference book set on his knees. With attention dropping, Blondel raised his voice, causing the whispers to grow louder as he moved onto his favorite subject: the forthcoming generation of satellites responsible, among other things, for mapping the bottom of the seas, evaluating the energy of waves, the drift of the continental plates and the direction of the wind.

His speech finished, everyone stood up speaking several decibel levels higher, I went down the aisle toward the stage where Blondel was sullenly arranging his papers. Friends and colleagues had gathered around him, his assistant Vuarcheix, Lucie, to whom I gave a distant smile, then Poecile the engineer who was claiming, oh come on, it wasn't that bad. Forget it, grumbled Blondel without having seen me, it's obvious they don't give a damn. The funding won't be coming in this year. He went on shuffling his papers like a giant deck of cards, acting as if he'd folded his hand, lost the game. There's still Cosmo, pointed out Vuarcheix, we've still got Cosmo.

Blondel shrugged his shoulders, I knew as well as he did what the situation was with the Cosmo satellite, the first of the environmentalist machines put into orbit four years earlier. After its last breakdown, irreparable from the ground, Cosmo now transmitted little more than incomplete data and misaligned photos, frequently blurred. I coughed. Ah, said Blondel, you're here too. You saw how little they care. Normal with all our launch failures, I noted, all of our explosions. An explosion makes us look ridiculous. But things'll work out, I went on, we'll manage to bounce back. May God keep you in his favor, sighed Blondel as he turned toward Lucie, who smiled at me again. Are you eating with us? Guys night out, he specified, unfortunately Lucie has to leave us. Thanks, I replied, but no.

I started toward the door.

After my departure, around ten o'clock, Blondel stopped by Poecile's office to make a call. Séguret, he said, it's me. Were you able to check on the injection valves? We're on it, we're on it, assured Séguret. We'll figure it out. Okay, said Blondel, is Meyer still there? At this hour? said Séguret. Hold on, I'll go check.

Muffling the receiver with his hand, Séguret the engineer turned toward an immense desk at the end of the room, toward another engineer, large-sized, proportionate to the desk over which he was leaning.

Meyer, said Séguret, Blondel's asking for you. Are you here?

2

THE SIMOOM, AN EXTREMELY hot wind, rises up in gusts in the south of Saharan Morocco, producing compact, burning, sharp, deafening tornados that conceal the sun and chap the Bedouin. The simoom reshapes the desert, redresses the oases, expropriates the dunes, the scattered sand deeply embedding itself nearly everywhere: beneath the Bedouin's fingernail, inside both the Tuareg's turban and the dromedary's anus.

The Tuareg, covered in blue, sits quietly on the hump of his animal. Next to him, fossilized beneath the storm, three other Tuaregs wait for it to settle while the sand goes on building a pedestal of rock dust around the animals' ankles. When the youngest of the Tuaregs, panicking, screams that he's sinking and that things are taking a turn for the worst, his elders say nothing in response. Beneath their protective covering, they must not have heard the novice's voice. Because all around them the sandstorm squeals wildly.

Better instructed than the young camel rider, his elders know that the phenomenon originates at the heart of the continent, that a north wind from central Africa rips through the great northern desert every so often, where it boils the barren vastness and transports the resulting froth across the sea. Releasing ballast to the water's surface—like a hot air balloon carrying sandbags from the Grand Erg—shaking the titanium of a passing Boeing, the desert flies toward Europe, where it goes to powder the northwest, to smooth out the beaches and hurl grains of sand into gears and machinery.

Moving toward the north, the Moroccan flying carpet reaches Paris in the middle of the night, scattering itself uniformly throughout the city, not forgetting, of course, the Moroccan district, toward Stalingrad after rue de Tanger: it covers Morocco street, Morocco square, and the impasse of Morocco, at the end of which resides Louis Meyer, an astigmatic man and a graduate of the École Polytechnique, forty-nine years old last Thursday, a specialist in ceramic engines. An unfaithful man divorced by his ex-wife, born Victoria Salvador on the same day as the invention of the transistor radio. A lonely and overworked man who, for his birthday, is going to treat himself to a relaxing week at the beach.

The sun is rising, Meyer packs his bags. Proceeds methodically: from top to bottom of the body then from interior to exterior of the being, from sunhat to flip-flops then from aspirin to sunblock. That looks like everything, what could I be forgetting? Meyer looks around himself at the order reigning over the few accessories of his life, four or five priceless pieces of furniture, including a large, unsightly couch, covered with a checkerboard fabric. A portable television, a commemorative radio. Against a wall five hundred books pile up and spill into one another, complement and contradict each other in several different languages over points on flight mechanics, solid-state physics, and fluid dynamics.

Meyer is methodical but his gaze, sometimes, drifts beyond the horizon of things to do—either he replays a traumatic scene from his divorce or he anticipates the coming week of vacation at Nicole's. Depending on which one, his eyes settle accordingly on one of the two concave ektachromes leaning against the wall on the radiator cover; one shows the chateau d'If, the other is an overexposed American map from Victoria, last name Salvador then ex-Meyer.

Meyer closes his bag and takes a breath. Let's go, he says out loud before switching off the gas and water, then locking the door. He comes out of the building carrying two travel bags, his removable car radio tucked beneath his arm. The impasse of Morocco has grown a shade yellower during the night, now coated in a fine layer of sand, which softens sounds, muffles the world, aerates the air, produces a Sunday-like silence reminiscent of snow beneath a cold sun; and like in the snow, footprints can be seen.

The cars parked in the impasse seem empty but on their rear dashes several folded newspapers can be made out, as well as maps and route planners, umbrellas and catalogues, Kleenex boxes and little fans or, perhaps, a faded decorative stuffed animal, a green hat, a green glove, a printout of computer code, a pocket edition of an Annabel Buffet novel, sometimes more than one or two of these things at the same time. Whatever the case, they're difficult to see behind the windows, veiled by the Sahara's film, made up with a blush that dulls the brightness. Meyer runs a rag over his car's windows, climbs inside and then slams the door. Ignition, engine, seatbelt, first gear, radio. Then, suddenly, he's unsure if he shut off his electricity.

He exits the car, reenters his building while swearing beneath his breath. Reaching the door of his apartment, he hears the telephone ringing all alone behind the door, rapid hypotheses take shape as he looks for his key: who could be calling at this hour? Martine obviously not. Monique not yet, Francoise surely not. Couldn't be Mom. Who else? Victoria.

3

ABSOLUTELY NOT VICTORIA, of course not, idiot. No sign of her for two years as you're well aware of. No, it's Blondel at the other end, calling back about the injection valves. It's Blondel who's always up to something, up every day before daybreak: no faults or weaknesses to be found in this man besides a repugnant and stumpy dog named Dakota, a supposed sub-brand of a bull terrier, more likely a crossbreed between a rat terrier and a rat.

— Tried to reach you last evening, said Blondel, but you'd already left. We've fixed the problem with the propellant output, I think. Vuarcheix came up with the idea. Simple enough, all we had to do was recalibrate the opening on the valve outlet.

— Good thinking, acknowledges Meyer.

— Nothing's ever truly fixed though, let's not forget. The umbilical connectors, the turbopumps. All those little things that never seem to get resolved.

Meyer's fingers drum out a rhythm on the telephone's shelf: this means that I'm no longer here, he says. I'm already on my way out. Yes, recalls Blondel, your vacation, that's right. I forgot. Well, I'll let you go, he says before hanging up and then dialing the ministry's number on his other phone while, panting below his desk, Dakota the animal fidgets about weakly, producing prodigious amounts of gas and drool.

Having finally shut off the electricity to his apartment, Meyer started off again; thirty minutes later as he was leaving Paris, anticipating a single stop for coffee and gas somewhere around Beaune, the sun was shining. As usual, the traffic was dense and fitful, although maybe even more dense and fitful than usual; from the very outset a large proportion of damaged cars could be seen washed up on the shoulders.

Most had only suffered a little surface damage, but three of them, overturned on their sides, were staging the performance of white nurse coats and cold blood beneath the ultramarine sky, complemented by the equally tricolored vehicles: pale ambulances, scarlet tow trucks, and the royal blue vans of the gendarmerie. Sorrowful actors came and went among all this, exasperatedly waving forms while pointing to this bruised part of their anatomy, that bruised part of their vehicle.

On the packed lanes of the freeway, the drivers seemed tense, as if waiting for everything to suddenly explode; braking to better catch the spectacle's highlights, they created one of those exuberant, feverish traffic jams, radiant with curse words and horns, flashing headlights, crunching gearboxes and cracked windshields, dented bumpers surrounded by the roaring of caged-in cylinders. Meyer decided to drive in the right-hand lane, fearing the hostile energy of the other drivers, who eventually calmed down, progressively, with the passing of kilometers: a lighter consistency of traffic, a more relaxed atmosphere among the vehicles. But also less exciting.

Every work morning of the year, Louis Meyer takes the A1 freeway west toward his laboratory. The one that goes south, at the moment, shouldn't be any big change: all these six-lane roads look the same, you drive along each one identically. And yet, the one that leads to salaried employment doesn't have the same flavor as the one that grants paid vacation, the mood is somehow different. It's the same every morning when getting dressed: though the motions are the same, the enthusiasm and state of mind vary depending on whether Meyer dons overalls or slips on his Bermuda shorts, whether he puts on espadrilles or protective bootees.

But this feeling of vacation never sufficiently diminishes the boredom of the freeway: to distract himself Meyer would sing a little, talk to himself sometimes in an extremely loud voice, scream out the answers to quiz shows on the radio. Then, tired of his own noise, with one hand and one eye he would launch into an inventory of the glove box. But when a small bracelet made of blue and yellow braided cotton suddenly appeared from the back of the glove box, forgotten there for years, a suddenly chilled Meyer would slam it shut while briskly accelerating. A little speed, come on, to help take your mind off things.

Other objects left in his apartment by Victoria rushed through his mind, three or four stockings, two worn-out T-shirts and some makeup accessories, little brushes losing their bristles, vials of lotion, containers of crumbling foundation; all this had been thrown out without any real difficulty. It'd been more difficult with two pairs of black underwear discovered much later, well after her departure, during a day of big rearrangement in the deepest stratum of the hall closet: one high, one low, delicate anatomic landmarks, very expressive, very soul-stirring, very difficult to throw away, but he'd managed to get rid of them all the same. He'd managed to get rid of them all the same. Would only keep, pinned up on a wall in the kitchen, a portrait of a brunette woman who'd always reminded him of Victoria (although she'd been blonde), a photograph by Cindy Sherman entitled *Untitled Film Still #7.*

The bracelet is still twirling through his fingers when his car passes the exit for Avallon, he's well aware that his thoughts shouldn't be going in this direction. Even if the story of Louis Meyer and Victoria Salvador had begun with a long kiss, one of those very long kisses that makes history, defines an era, that changes your way of breathing and your vision of the world forever. They'd seen no one else in the six weeks that'd followed, their life for forty days reduced to sex, sleeping, sex, sleeping, sex, sleeping—but there's more to life than just sleeping and sex, you also have to wake up and go to work, to make money that will allow you to buy things to drink and things to eat, flowers, and clothing that get ripped feverishly away to have sex one more time before going back to sleep.

When love is so deep, sometimes you get a little overwhelmed; behind the star in the foreground appear so many other blonde girls, at first indistinct among the scenery, discreetly crossing through the shot at the back, as if the world wanted to remind you that it's filled with all these other walk-on actresses. Blondes with whom Meyer goes to linger a little bit longer every day, taking stock of them until Victoria, in turn, goes out of focus. Until she decides that enough is enough.

But Meyer's mind shouldn't have gone in this direction either. To protect himself he'd concentrate on the landscape, reading whatever was within range: names of rest stops, gas prices, comments painted on the long vehicles, slogans attached to rear windows, Citroen recommends Elf, Austin-Rover prefers Castrol, NO to the chemical plant in Grez-en-Bouère! But so tenacious is nostalgia, so enduring is Meyer's regret, such a persistent couch grass, that by analogy these stickers eventually made him think of the small blue jaguar tattooed behind Victoria's shoulder. Then as he was passing a tow truck dragging a Peugeot filled with dismayed children (what could the problem be? the carburetor? the ignition?), he transposed his situation onto theirs, imagining himself as this Peugeot, the tow truck of his destiny pulling away his body and his sunken morale (so what's the problem? hypertension? overexertion?), and up until Lyon things would be particularly difficult.

Twenty kilometers before Lyon, his thoughts slow down and come to a standstill at the tollbooth: Louis Meyer kindly greets the employee. Holds out his ticket in a folded bill, takes his change, thanks the employee, kindly says goodbye. Floating rib in the body of the world, Meyer still makes an effort to be polite with tollbooth workers.

4

TWO HUNDRED KILOMETERS past Lyon, toward the beginning of the Vaucluse, above a flat landscape furnished on the right with three chimneys rising out of a breeder reactor, Meyer saw the line of black smoke.

A twisting vertical line drawn into the pale sky, a narrow column with a spirally top: at its base a yellow Mercedes was parked crookedly on the side of the road, straddling the emergency lane. From its hood escaped a stream of thick, gaseous sludge from which several sticky particles, substitutes for crushed insects, stuck to the windshields of passing cars. Which accelerated bravely toward the Mercedes, then moved past it as quickly as possible. Nothing heroic or especially altruistic about Meyer: if he brakes and accidently flips on his blinker, if he parks near the enormous cloud of smoke, it's less out of concern for his fellow man than for himself, more than anything else it's to take his mind off things.

A young woman stood near the Mercedes, long red hair and a matching out of season fur coat, a saggy, elegant purse hanging from her shoulder. From the interior of his car, which he didn't immediately get out of, Meyer could see only her backside, leaning toward the door and surrounded by smoke. Speaking from the depths of her hair into a telephone, whose line was angled through the lowered window, she held the receiver between three careful fingers and at a slight distance, as if it was the phone that was at risk of exploding. But she also appeared to be expressing

14

herself calmly, without the breathless disorder of an emergency call: although in principle Meyer intended to help her, at first he remained motionless behind his steering wheel, seized by a scruple, an incongruous concern not to disturb her, preferring to wait until she'd hung up.

The smoke, suddenly, changed color and consistency, becoming thicker and more opaque, a pure black bellowing out in rapid torrents. And still the young woman hadn't moved, forced now only to talk a little bit louder into her phone, probably, because on top of everything else a loud noise like a raspy bellow had started up, as if the engine had begun to boil. When a muffled draft-like explosion rang out, causing a large, delicate bouquet of bright yellow flames to bloom above the hood before immediately withering, Meyer decided that it was time, perhaps, to intervene.

He opens his door, gets out of the car. Admittedly this redhead's behavior makes him hesitate, baffles him, she seems to be taking her time in the heat of the disaster instead of running away; she hurls three more words into the telephone before leaning over toward the inside of her car to hang up. Having leisurely walked around to it, she takes two pieces of luggage out of her trunk, which she then sets on the ground. She also withdraws and unpins a small vermillion fire extinguisher, whose contents she goes to unload into the hood, still in no rush, with small elegant movements, as if spraying distilled water onto houseplants. She's insane, thinks Meyer. He begins running.

He's running, he's barely covered four or five meters when the fire revives in the Mercedes: acetylene green trim and iron gray center, high orange flames take hold of the vehicle and begin devouring it from the front, with a powerful throbbing like a flaring gasworks. But the young woman still seems unconcerned, she goes on sprinkling the fire with the delicate movements of a housewife, among the sharp stench of burning neoprene and Teflon, of melting paint and oil. Meyer has just reached her in the middle of the commotion. Without presenting himself

as manners would dictate, he screams something out that she
doesn't seem to hear and then grabs her forearm: move away, he
screams louder, get out of here. She turns around and takes back
her arm, a condescending movement of the chin, an icy glare
for the stranger. Move away, in the name of fucking God, the
stranger now shouts, forcibly taking hold of the young woman's
other arm, though not without difficulty because of her slipping
fur coat, and tries to pull her away to a safe distance from the
inferno.

And the other struggling imbecile drops her extinguisher,
the extinguisher falls on one of Meyer's feet, who then grimaces
through the tumult's crescendo: harsh rattling, furious banging,
bursting tires and window, exploding accessories and options,
then a gut-wrenching grating that signals the death of the car's
most essential components. But Meyer, dripping with sweat and
hearing nothing, pushes and pulls the young woman beyond the
horrible shitstorm while mumbling other vulgarities, orders her
to lie down as soon as it seems they're far enough away. Because
she continues to resist he knocks her over, flattens her to the
ground and collapses on top of her, his nose burying itself into
her fur coat's fragrance at the exact moment that every last drop
of premium gasoline contained within the car explodes.

The car explodes with a sound like a loud hacking cough,
short and somewhat disappointing but immediately followed
by a thousand joyous jingle bells of metal, glass, chrome, bolts
raining over and bouncing off the freeway, a storm of scrap
iron that passing drivers avoid with sudden jerks of the wheel,
brutal kicks to the pedals like vehicular organists. Everyone's
fled, silence returns. Meyer, nestled in, stays tucked away, nose
to eyes buried in the fur, in a complete almost post-coital wash.
Then without moving he opens an eye, mechanically looks over
the breeder reactor.

Behind the burned-out Mercedes and beyond a line of linden
trees, sits the nuclear power plant, a flat building flanked by
short-legged cylindrical buildings, capped with domes, a long

flat building overlooked by three giant chimneys. Power cables beaded with red and white balls run from tall lattice towers, while from the chimneys a stationary and delicate mass of celestial vapor escapes, immaculate, Himalayan. Still buried in the soft protection of fur, the driver below him, Meyer keeps his eyes on the power plant. With no desire to move. But he has to when the young woman, in a muffled voice, asks him if he wouldn't mind letting her get up.

Having dusted themselves off without looking at each other, they then moved toward the burned vehicle, toward its large yellow detached jaw. Gaping open and askew, the hood displayed mangled mechanical entrails, dislocated valves and pistons, radiator hoses dribbling grease and oil like the severed arteries of a cyborg. Meyer took a look at the vehicle's interior: steering wheel multiplied by eight, rearview mirror hanging like a tooth by a nerve. Sagging on its shaft, the stick shift's liquefied hand knob was like a rotten mushroom on its stalk; of the seats only the adjustable frames remained. Where are you going? inquired Meyer.

The young woman took out a Benson from her purse, lit it while looking over her car then turned toward him. If you want, he said, I can take you as far as Marseille.

5

BUT FIRST, AT THE YOUNG woman's request and under the pretext of obscure insurance clauses, Meyer would have to unscrew the blackened plates of the Mercedes, which the young woman then buried inside her saggy purse. Next he'd load two more pieces of baggage into the trunk, a suitcase and a vanity case made of auburn ostrich, while she settled into the front seat of the car, wordlessly puffing on another Benson.

She wouldn't say much more on the way to Marseille. He'd try several different openings, but all in vain; in response, he wouldn't receive much more than three reluctant monosyllables from the end of her lips, not even a couple of evasive gestures with the tips of her fingers, barely a glance in his direction. When he decided to introduce himself, for the sake at least of sharing his first name with her, the driver of the ex-Mercedes gave an automatic nod of the head, without offering her own identity. All right, let's call her Mercedes and leave it at that. Help your fellow man, thought Meyer, not without bitterness. Would you mind buckling your seatbelt, he'd suggest afterward, somewhat curtly.

Then he switched on the radio a bit too nervously, not asking for the young woman's opinion, running aground on a program of practical advice: a drawling voice emphasized that young children, because of their small size, are poorly visible to the drivers of heavy trucks. A bit too nervously again, he changed the station: a wailing jingle suggested that listeners take advantage, before it's too late, of super bargains at minimum prices offered by a GPO. Then, much too nervously, Meyer turned off the radio.

Complete silence until Marseille, no more distractions except when construction slowed down traffic, restricting it to a single lane: Meyer was then able to follow thirty shots of a pink-tinted movie, playing on a TV screen mounted next to the rearview mirror of a green car from Spain, behind which they crawled slowly enough for a third Benson. Mercedes extracted a pair of sunglasses from her fur coat. They were almost there.

Before the disaster, the entrance to Marseille consisted of several long and steep slopes on both sides of the freeway. Slopes adorned with faded housing estates, prefab town halls, an enormous pale hospital looming over a drizzle of roughcast wards, a fair number of vegetable gardens and plots of land waiting to be developed. Several fin de siècle villas with terraces and turrets, converted into institutes of social action or medical-psychological-pedagogical centers. Several more vacant lots, but also two or three superstores surrounded by fields of shopping carts. It was starting to get hot, the sun coated the panorama with a sticky air haunted by phantom odors from dissolved soap factories and bankrupt oil factories—a pungent and drab atmosphere where one doesn't sense the proximity to the sea, toward the level of which they were all the same descending. Meyer began sweating. Where can I drop you off?

With an undulation of shoulders and blades, keeping her elbows still while lifting herself up a little, Mercedes removed her fur coat, beneath which a bright green blouse, rather revealing, delivered a precise and precious idea of her bust. Anywhere, she said distractedly, near a taxi stand. Then as they were entering the suspended section of the freeway that leads to the city center above the quays, over the storage docks and dry docks, the excessively indifferent young woman bent toward the sea. Okay, thinks Meyer, what am I doing here?

Upset about being upset, suddenly impatient to get rid of her, he braked sharply at the first stand they came to, will this be okay for you. Without waiting for a response he opened his door, authoritatively removed the suitcase and vanity case from the trunk and set them carelessly onto the dirty sidewalk, deaf to the protests of the outraged ostrich. Mercedes, of course, took her time getting out of the car before distractedly coming over, her attention elsewhere, her fur coat thrown haphazardly over her arm. When she began to bend over for her luggage, Meyer, annoyed with his behavior, took the initiative despite himself, picked up the bags and held them out to her with a tight smile. But the young woman smiles back and against all expectations it's the most radiant smile in the world, suddenly shining on Meyer like a sentimental sunbeam, a continental sentiment filled with everything one waits for, everything one expects from the century. And now he should immediately, quickly and gently, jump aboard this smile, settle in and run off with it for the rest of his life—but, oh, the girl's gone.

To reach Nicole's house, all he had to do was maintain a simple east-south-east course, parallel to the coast. But the sun, the heat, the lack of a map, and Mercedes's smile all lead to a flustered Meyer losing his way. At first getting lost in the very center of town, then wandering hopelessly toward its outskirts: the bars grew scarcer along with the grocery shops, the city streets turned into country roads and then grew narrower, winding and crossed by drifting gangs of derelict dogs, gyrovagues without identification tags.

Lost and acknowledging his mistake, Meyer's efforts to correct it only served to make it worse, like when you strangle to death a knot that you'd meant to untie: right before his eyes the suburbs were falling away. At the end of a shoulderless road, a low gray structure appeared that might have been a temporary housing project. At the end of another, three feral caravans were grouped together, covered in bright fabrics and crooked antennas. Fewer and fewer residences, sometimes the deserted campus of a civil engineering firm or a warehouse watched over by another class of dogs, domesticated, rallied together around the order of articulated language, better fed but not having as much fun. Then the landscape began to present authentic rural lots, more or less preserved: little zones of vegetable cultivation, silos, small farms flanked by their corresponding yards. Definitely off route, Meyer stopped in front of one to ask for directions.

His car parked on the side of the road, half of one tire in the ditch, Meyer approached the gate. At a first glance nothing in the yard besides a plane tree sitting at its center. Then Meyer made out the gleaming head and top half of an insane horse in the shadows of a stall, a powerful foaming beast whose eyes were frozen with terror and who, suddenly rearing up, began to beat his front hooves against the door of his stall. The repetitive impact of the hooves rang out ominously before Meyer noticed, from several other indications, that a nervous atmosphere hung over the farmyard: shivering in a tight row, the chickens were perched on one of the plane tree's branches while several extremely stressed ducks had moved into the branch above, far from the muddy circle of water at whose edge, stares frozen and hair standing up, four pigs appeared to be in a state of shock. There didn't seem to be a precise source of fear—poor treatment, the butcher's boy, microwave ovens—so much as a deep, unspecified malaise. Only two young beige and gray dogs, sprawled out at the entrance of the farmhouse, still seemed at peace.

After Meyer had knocked twice against the screen door's frame, a kind-looking farmer appeared. In a voice hinting at the end of a nap and Catalonia, he cheerfully gave directions to the ocean. Then, the horse having once again started to kick like a huge defective mechanical toy, the two languid dogs near the door suddenly got up, stiff on the tips of their flaking toenails. Trembling, they began howling in harmony, accompanied off-camera by their neighborhood congeners, guard dogs and homeless dogs, German shepherds and outlaw bastards. Furrowing unconcerned eyebrows, the farmer bent over to calm them in his mother tongue, slowly they flattened out with a whimper. What's wrong with them? said Meyer. Maybe a storm, the farmer guessed. They get like this sometimes before they fall. Sometimes. You think you'll be able to find your way? Yes, said Meyer, thank you. An hour later, beneath a sky that could be described as anything but stormy, he pulled up in front of Nicole's.

6

HE'D MET NICOLE WHEN HE was nothing more than a man abandoned by Victoria, one of those classic lonely types who analyze the lyrics of sad love songs playing on the bathroom radio, staring at themselves in the mirror from the depths of a bathrobe, brushing their teeth to the point of blood for no one. Nicole had been very helpful in consoling Meyer at the end of the Victorian era, then when things had smoothed out they'd gone on being only occasional lovers, should the opportunity arise, not too far from an excessively empty bed after two or three drinks put down excessively fast.

But not now. Now Meyer regularly comes down to spend several days of vacation in Nicole's house, a bleached straw-colored villa, medium-sized, three bedrooms above a big living room that leads onto a flowery terrace filled with columbines, irises, wood sorrels. He always stays in the same cramped bedroom that looks out onto the sea, separated from a minuscule shower room by a treacherous step, potentially jaw-breaking when one isn't aware of it. Meyer's well aware of it. Like a duck in water at the little parties Nicole hosts two or three times per week, each time he's spoilt for choice from the buzzing, blooming, polychrome gathering of young women.

You don't want to take a shower? Nicole suggests, you're not a little hungry? You don't want me to make you something light,

simple, and quick? Maybe a soft-boiled egg, come on. Fine, said
Meyer modestly, I'd like that very much but I wouldn't want
to be a burden. Let's go, Nicole cries out as she submerges two
eggs into a pot of boiling water. Now, my little darlings, you're
going to cook.

Meyer watches her a moment then takes his glass, in which
spins an ice cube, and stretches out on the terrace, nestled in a
chaise longue; the afternoon is drawing to a close. A record of
soft tropical music plays at a low volume, a zephyr brings in a
little sea air, the iris and the mock-orange exude slowly, deeply,
far away from wars and the crash of bombs, from the rattle of
automatic weapons, of hand grenades and heavy artillery; neither
tears nor terror between the pots of verbena, the striped cruise
ships, the spotted beach umbrellas; the peace. Two iron bracelets
hold up the damaged concrete of a pillar on the terrace.

Nicole, however, speaks, giving fast motion news about
Georges, whom she left for a certain Bill, I want you to meet Bill,
of Chantal who's lost pleasure in everything since Fred moved in
with Jean-René, of Pierre-Paul and Marie-Cécile, Youssouf and
everyone else, in any case you'll see them this evening. Nicole
also talks about the weather, particularly muggy these last two
days, are you sure you don't feel like taking a shower, really?
Meyer doesn't respond, Meyer walks the ends of his fingers over
his moist cheeks, going against the grain, a straw mat.

He gets up, walks toward the railing and takes in the panorama. In the distance: the Mediterranean. To the left: three
white stone cliffs chase one another out toward the sea, three
circus tents on which a dozen or so apartment towers, built at
their base, take the place of stakes; and a new tower is under
construction, watched over by two lofty cranes, one green, one
yellow. Between here and there stretches an oval racecourse,
not far from the beach, which is only a ten-minute walk away.
Silently, Meyer replays Mercedes's smile while Nicole carries on
with the inventory of invited friends. When will they be here?
he asks absentmindedly.

By ten o'clock they were all there: the Barabino brothers (Georges is an international referee, Pierre-Paul a product designer), Marie-Cécile and Youssouf (who took over the restaurant on the cape with Mickey), Dr. Braun and Black his Labrador, Jany Laborde in a dark black bustier accompanied by her little sister Sandrine Laborde in a green bodysuit (and who is making her debut, this evening, in the social circle), Dédé Gomez (scaffolder, frequenter of parties), and finally Chantal who, it's true, doesn't seem to be doing so well. A gravitational core of close friends around which float yet more satellites. The certain Bill had yet to show up, but he figured among the satellites of charming people. The anatomy of a bubbly blonde, in particular, quickly caught Louis Meyer's attention, he wanted to know immediately who it was: Cynthia, a model, opal dots in her ears, golden ankle bracelet. Behind each of these attributes, Meyer immediately sniffs out the off-notes—fake first name, scattered employment history, superficial—but still he begins with this young woman while keeping his eye on another (Marion Morhange, the niece of Dr. Braun).

Out on the terrace, whose cement floor was releasing layers of the suffocating heat stored up throughout the day, Meyer duly engaged in conversation with the artificial satellite, standing as closely as possible. Several drops of alcohol were still missing from the guests' blood levels, for the moment nobody was opening up to dance. The music thus remained low, for the time being kept to the background, restrained to a minimal volume but waiting for the slightest movement, for the most subtle shake of the hips, pressed up against its starting block, ready for anything. The ocean was just a bit too far and a bit too calm for them to make out the noise of its waves, but from the surrounding green oak trees bands of insects grazed the air, making it itch every last inch of itself, in effusions of varying intensity that sometimes drowned out the conversations. Then from behind the curtain rose up the four distinctive beats of a Triumph Bonneville 650, a plump bicylindrical throbbing that can only be found in old English cycles, which eventually worked its way in slow motion to a standstill beneath the terrace, switching off after a final growl of the accelerator thrown out into the night. Bill, I suppose. Meyer followed Cynthia to the railing.

Bent over its frame in the warm halo of a streetlamp, an athletic man was calmly locking the anti-theft device. From a distance, dressed in red tracksuit pants with a white side stripe and a T-shirt with the noun EMERGENCY heat-pressed in red onto a white background, he embodied the idea of the heroic lifeguard or firefighter, the allegory of first aid. His teeth flashed when, with a large movement, he waved to Nicole, who was delighted to see him jog up the sloping entrance to the villa.

Commotion when a moment later the athlete appeared on the terrace, big shoulders and big jaw, big smile and a commanding voice, high-top sneakers with complicated laces: immediately all the girls were hanging suspended and starstruck from his powerful neck. When Nicole then came over to introduce Meyer to Bill, just a moment of inattention sufficed to make Cynthia disappear. The moment after, nearby, Meyer saw her monopolized by a squat and stocky boy, shorter than her and wearing a glazed chestnut jacket—it's always important to keep a close eye on this kind of satellite, ready to float out of orbit the second your attention wavers, when your telescope starts focusing on anything else.

Meyer shook Bill's hand, withdrawing it intact before moving on to Marion Morhange, another celestial body spotted higher up. A tall beautiful young brunette tucked into a long and beautiful red dress, a very nice fit without the smallest pocket of air, not the slightest sign of hesitation in either her eyes or her smile: immediately they felt comfortable together, immediately he felt he knew Marion whose grounded demeanor and natural laugh no doubt indicated the appétit of an ogre, the sleep of an angel, an iron constitution. Of course Meyer, usually, prefers indirect and difficult to interpret, the coded locks instead of the wide-open vaults, but the Marion system also has its good points. We'll see.

After a little conversation, Cynthia passed nearby and smiled to Meyer on her way out, followed by the stocky boy. You're already leaving, a surprised Meyer asked politely, ignoring the iced chestnut stare. Standard dialogue, offer of a phone call: since the young woman didn't seem opposed to the idea, Meyer looked in his jacket for something to write on, quickly finding a Bic but no paper. On a table, behind a pyramid of glasses, was a basket of citrus fruit from which Cynthia took a piece, writing a royal blue number on a yellow lemon that Meyer tucked away in his pocket with a smile. Then, during the time dedicated to this exchange, Marion Morhange had left as well.

Outcome of these poorly planned attempts: toward midnight Meyer found himself alone again. Pouring himself a drink and then finding himself alone with the drink, passing from one group to another without saying more than a couple of words. Sufficiently oxidized by now, several of the party's younger members were dancing the pogo, Meyer was happy to stay on the sidelines. In search of ice cubes he made his way to the presently deserted kitchen, lifting without tasting the first stratum of an abandoned club sandwich, just to look, leaning out the window that looked out behind the house: nothing to see there either except a small construction site in the darkness, the silhouette of an orange excavator nosed up against a pile of purple rocks. A noise coming from behind made him turn around: Marion had just come in looking as if she was halfheartedly searching for something. After he offered, indicating his own glass, to make her a gin and tonic, she responded that she was more in the mood for a sparkling water or soda, a Coke, something along those lines. Meyer stepped aside to open the fridge for her, chivalrously, as if it were a car door, stocked inside with lots of things along those lines.

— On second thought, she said while turning toward him. Maybe a lemonade.

— No problem, Meyer said calmly, withdrawing the

numbered lemon from his pocket, cutting it in two, pressing it, then serving it in a large glass to the young woman.

And then it's common knowledge that people often end up kissing in kitchens, at this kind of party—fiery kisses burn on the stove, stick to the fridge, tip over into the sink, it's well known. People improvise quick, off-the-cusp little kisses to be snacked on standing up, unembellished and simple, though they can also be endlessly simmered, feature-length embraces that get savored leisurely. Normally these kisses then get arranged on a tray and quickly carried off into a bedroom or some other private, out-of-the-way place, so they can be sampled more freely and eaten until you're stuffed—what the young woman had probably been hoping for, instead of Meyer offering to go for a stroll on the beach.

Already later than one in the morning, the party would soon be coming to an end, most people had already gone but some ten or so partygoers would stay in the chaise lounges on the terrace, maybe until daybreak, speaking softly of things which, unable to withstand the dazzle of the sun, would no longer exist, tomorrow, in their memories. Meyer and the young woman made their way down the steep, winding one-way path bordered by conifers and gates, each gate with a trash can and each trash can with a cat. Brother cats of the dogs seen in the suburbs: stray, suspicious and bad tempered, psychopathic. Meyer gently turned around a memory of ice cubes in his glass, his other hand on Marion's hip. At the bottom of the hill, the path widened out into a small delta grafted onto the six-lane corniche.

Above the ocean a vague hint of brightness, a first tear in the darkness, a run in the weft of the black sky, wasn't enough to provide a clear view of the beach or of the exact nature, scattered across the sand, of its waste. Tops of Ambre Solaire sunscreen and Carlsberg bottle caps, plastic bags, driftwood. Silhouettes of a sextet of seagulls quarreling over who would be first to rip apart some shapeless item. The seagulls dispersed as Meyer approached and bent over the item, still unable to identify it. A kind of frothy sponge halfway between an animal and a vegetable, even between the organic and the manufactured: corrupted cadaver, chemical lump, a knot of algae or something like that. Meyer stood up, noticed the glass in his hand, a quick lukewarm gulp and a quick grimace. With the edge of his foot, before the scowling stares of the seagulls lingering nearby, he returned the thing to its natural environment, a compound of three-fourths still water, salted to 29 g/l, and one-fourth waste water, with two drops of hydrocarbons, a handful of bacteria, E. coli and vibrio, a bit of nitrate, a pinch of phosphate as well as a zest of fertilizer, shake well, serve at 20 degrees centigrade; Meyer threw the end of his drink into the cocktail, differentiating his formula with a quarter-tone of gin.

Shoes in hand, Marion walked through the expansive, dissipating waves, who stuck out long flat effervescent tongues as they died. Meyer joined her: beaches at night, for kissing, are almost as good as kitchens. Marion closed her eyes for the duration, Meyer not entirely. The sky would still be dark for a long time before giving way to the charcoal, the sandstone, the slate, the pearl pink that precede the first rays of light. Then, as if half-opening, a large bright flash invaded it for just an instant, radiating it for the time of a heartbeat. A silent flash of lightning, then the immediately restored night. Did you see that? said Meyer. The flash. The lightning. You didn't see? No, said Marion softly, are you sure? I don't know, said Meyer, maybe not. Maybe it's just me. A dizzy spell. It happens from time to time.

7

Nine o'clock in the morning, ringing of the telephone. I pick up immediately. Blondel.

A rather depressed Blondel complaining as always about how no one wanted to listen to him at the agency, that they weren't giving enough attention to the environmental program. I consoled him as best I could but cut the call short.

Didn't have much more planned than the previous Monday. I considered tidying up a bit around the house, but this forced idleness had already led me to arranging everything several times over. Not really in the mood to go out for the moment. I tried to call Jacqueline: busy. Then my attention went to Titov, who, as usual, was sleeping peacefully in his corner. Few creatures as calm as this one, few among them who sleep so often, so long. Titov is so peaceful and so well-mannered that, as always, I'd left the door of his little room open. Well-mannered but not very entertaining: he made gentle little turns in his sleep, every so often letting out some small sound. Nothing very entertaining.

Passing through the apartment, first inspecting my collection of shirts, then filing some papers already filed a hundred times, I happened upon the large box of Ilford photographic paper where I store old pictures. I don't have that many, certainly less than my colleagues burdened with family, but I decided to sort through them all the same. Personal photos on one side, professionals on the other. Among the latter I found the one

Max had used for my portrait, as displayed at Pontarlier's. In
another box I keep a pile of copies, provided by the agency, of
the same photo. It's what I use when asked for a signed picture,
which, two or three times per year, some young boy works up
the courage to do.

Personal side, no shortage of pictures showing women in my
company, sometimes not in my company, rarely in the company
of a third. Jacqueline, who I see more often than the others, was
likewise more frequently portrayed. At the beach, in the snow,
in the shower, in the street. With me at Borobudur, alongside
the Amur River with me again, the only two times we ever went
on vacation together—each time a catastrophe. But also in my
possession, most notably, were shots much more moving and
distinguished, certain ones that she doesn't even know about,
several pictures of Lucie. On a research trip, at the agency, at a
conference or in the street. I looked through them.

Sorting all this out took up no time at all.

Afterward I conceived then rejected a plan to call, one after
another, all the other girls to be found smiling in my photos.
At Jacqueline's, in any case, the line was still busy. I hesitated a
moment before calling Lucie at her desk but, after I'd made up
my mind, her secretary informed me that she'd been away for
several days.

Not easy, for a guy like me, to be forced to stay at home.
I decided to go out to my terrace and have a look at the sky,
which had become very pale. With a little something new to
the south: unusual reddish streaks that brought to mind a form
of eczema, a dermatitis or something like that. Not so pretty. I
went, for lack of anything better to do, to get the home trainer
from my bedroom and carried it out onto the terrace. Settled
on top of its sliding seat, I spent the morning tugging on its
springs, pushing on the machine's jointed levers, coming and
going along its tracks, rowing, bench press, flex, maintenance
of biceps and triceps brachii, work on the quadriceps femoris.
Abdominals, abdominals.

8

TEN O'CLOCK IN THE MORNING. Consider for me this individual who wakes up in a panic, confused about why he's just been torn out of his dream—a nasty story about scaffolding or scaffold, about a dwarf consulting blueprints from over his shoulder—unsure where exactly he is, in what bed, in which of the two hundred and fifty beds from his life. He opens an eye, he recognizes his bedroom at Nicole's, reminds himself of its features—the white wood of the furniture and the light pink wallpaper, sky and marine blues behind the window, and finally the little jaw-breaking step that adds a bit of adventure to the shower room's entrance. He remains motionless but his hand reaches out in a slow exploration of the sheet's surface, until the tips of his fingers meet someone else's skin: now it's Marion's features that he thinks back to. He opens his other eye and turns toward the sleeping young woman, catches sight of a small oval mark from a cutireaction test on her shoulder, large as a fingerprint and wavy as a nutshell.

Shutting his eyes again, reassured by the durability of the world, he singles out just then what's awoken him: it's a boiling sound from the nervous ocean, as present as an effervescent aspirin bubbling, within arm's reach, in a glass on the nightstand—and for that matter this aspirin, by the way, Meyer wouldn't turn it down. It's a rumbling of water under pressure, strangely close, not unlike the hum of running water, a borborygmus of pipes in

32

the house's stomach. Too exhausted to be astonished, to go look for that pill, and vaguely calmed by this natural sound, Meyer falls asleep again on his back.

But watch him again, an hour later, barely half-opening an eyelid when Marion gets up and goes toward the shower room. Maybe it'd be good to react, to show a little presence of mind, to warn the young woman about the perils of her journey. But Meyer, much too foolish, barely mumbles from the bottom of his pillow, Ook out for the st, sound of a fall, too late.

Later, on the terrace, surrounded by empty glasses and full ashtrays, Meyer and Marion buttered toast beneath a parasol. Silence from the inside of the villa, Nicole was probably still asleep, Meyer couldn't remember if Bill had stayed. Beneath the eczema of cicadas devouring the hot air and the melancholic cries of seagulls in withdrawal, the breakfast produced its own small soft bursts of sound, fracturing of toast and breaking of biscuit, dull earthenware-stainless steel percussions. Yawns and whispers. Then, after the young woman had looked almost everywhere for her purse, Meyer spent a moment alone on the terrace, looking out over the ocean, the hills, the racetrack, wearing a red mesh bucket hat found beneath a deckchair.

Another hour later, Meyer had left his car in the shade of the train station, extracted the radio from its compartment. Presently, the radio at the end of his arm, he descended the monumental stairway. Numerous colonial allegories weighed down the stairs, which were framed by two very tall palm dates standing at attention. Uncomfortable playing this regulatory miscasting, so far from their casual, undulating calling, disappointed that their exotic essence hadn't been put to better use, the palm trees withered where they stood, trapped without any other prospects while Meyer, much more mobile, drew up a small list of errands to run in the city—buy sandals, postcards, and have a drink on the harbor at the Locarno, at the San Remo. Halfway down the stairs, he could see the network of roads sliding gently down toward sea level. At the bottom of the

hundred steps he found himself on boulevard d'Athènes, moving
past a large number of North Africans, Central Africans, fewer
Far than Near Easterners, then two French sexagenarian twins
identically permed and made-up, wearing the same pink tracksuit but not quite the same brand of sneakers—always rather
touching, twins, especially with a bit of age.

Meyer went down boulevard d'Athènes, lingering as usual
in the wake of passing women—it's a little game, each time, to
identify their perfume. Meyer's not unfamiliar with the dosage,
the usage, the chemistry of each one of these perfumes on any
particular skin type: how Calèche changes on a brunette, Vol de
Nuit on a fake blonde, Joy on a divorced redhead, Je Reviens on
an elated widow. Eyes half-closed, his nose cutting through the
fragrant air like an icebreaker, he forms his hypotheses before
turning to verify.

In a recess off boulevard d'Athènes, after the corner of rue
des Convalescents, Meyer knew he'd find the Hotel Sudan,
in front of which he then spent several seconds of hesitation.
Perhaps Élizabeth had changed, left her bedroom on the fifth
floor to go find a husband, but then again perhaps she might
welcome him in an old green kimono, half-opening a suspicious door blackened by footprints, ordering him in a low and
nervous voice to get the hell out of here or I'll call the cops.
The hotel, in any case, hadn't changed at all, with its wealth of
obsolete conveniences and comforts—running water, private
dining rooms—engraved on a black oval screwed in near the
entrance, but the old mismatched blinds, the windows fixed up
with electrical tape, with Band-Aids, sometimes a plastic bag
stretched out in their place, made it clear that the hotel's luck
had run out. On the fifth floor and to the left, he recognized a
pair of window curtains, a cheerful Senegalese fabric that had
depicted, in its glory days, proud lions and haughty tigers on
a bright blue and blood-red background, radiant and glowing,
but which three years of solar erosion had dampened, rendered

morose, its background now pearl gray and antique pink, all of
its wildcats tamed, domesticated, hunchbacked. Meyer pushed
open the door of the hotel anyway.

In the shadow of a comatose ficus, the man at reception was
flipping through a newspaper beneath a twelve-speed fan that
you might expect to see in India. Meyer deciphered the title of an
article (*THE MAX CREMIEUX CUP: A More than Honorable
Defeat*) before coughing lightly, which caused the man to look
up with the severity of a Pentecostal stretcher-bearer—no more
than thirty, no more than a thousand flimsy hairs camping
out in the open on the slopes of his temples. A chrome-plated
ceiling light sent a fluorescent glare over the skulls of both the
receptionist (bald) and Meyer (parted on the side), who, while
continuing to skim the newspaper in reverse (*Miramas: In Search
of the Maniac*), asked if by chance a mademoiselle Élizabeth Frise
still lived here. Room 48 on the fifth floor, stated the stretcher-bearer. So nothing had changed in over a thousand days.

Flaking a bit here, fading a bit there, furnished with pale
photos of the Opéra, of the château d'If and the porte d'Aix
in the fifties, the stairwell was layered with a burgundy plush,
the palmette-patterned red and black carpet covering its steps
up to the third floor before giving way to fringed sisal. Almost
to room 48, Meyer thought back on Élizabeth, their embraces,
their goodbyes: in apnea from kissing, her shoved up against him
in a brand new green kimono, him delegating his fingers behind
the scenes of the delicate piece of clothing, one May morning
in front of this door upon which he now knocked twice. Softly.

She hadn't changed all that much, still attractive beneath
her small stripe-print dress—a pattern from *Neue Mode* over
a piece of fabric bought on sale at Ben Textile. It's me, Meyer
said flatly. I see that, she said without any apparent surprise.
Do you want to come in? A cautious glance from Meyer over
what could be seen, from the landing, in the bedroom behind
Élizabeth, in the softened light coming in through a curtain

covered with toothless felines: a table and a chair, a worn-in
men's jacket hanging over the chair's back, a secondhand bouquet on the table, three withered irises beneath crumpled cello-
phane. Lowering his voice, he said that he was passing by and
had thought: that he should've called ahead but he'd thought;
well, more than anything else he didn't want to be a disturbance.

But too late: from a blind spot in the room rose up the hacking of a throat and then the creaking of bedsprings, then a
sorrowful-eyed man appeared behind Elizabeth. Not short on
muscle, not lacking in body hair, black knee socks and white
underwear. A friend, said Elizabeth without moving. What
friend? Meyer immediately wonders. Him? Me? The other guy
held up a voluminous hand and took the liberty to introduce
himself. Quantity surveyor seeking employment, his earthly goal
was to make Élizabeth happy and to see to it that no one ever
comes to bother her again, ever. But he could tell right away that
Meyer wasn't the kind of person who'd try to bother Élizabeth,
he could see it clearly, he also invited him to call him by his first
name, Drajan, then to drink the end of this Slivovitz with them,
brought straight from over there.

A little early for Meyer, but there was a risk that Drajan, as
good-humored as he may have seemed, might take offense to a
refusal. The pain in his eyes could indicate the banal as well as
the worst, maternal deficiency or an upset stomach, horror of the
void or running low on filtered Gitanes. Prudence with this type
of man whose heavy, spontaneous kindness threatens, just below
the surface, to reverse at the slightest disturbance. Great, he said,
kind of you to offer. Just a small glass and then I'll be off.

Not quite so small in the end, however, it'd end up being two
glasses and then one for the road. Meyer's head is spinning as he
leaves the Hotel Sudan, himself not very happy with himself, he
hazily thinks over the details of his errands beneath a sun that's
not joking around, the radio weighs a quintal at the end of this
arm. Under the zenithal shower, toward the harbor, he follows
the slope of the streets, drifts along with no other guide than

the incline. Reaching the Palais de la Bourse he finds himself engulfed, a passive passerby, into a small pedestrian turbulence, right in front of a mall: suddenly carried away by this unstoppable motion, an insect on the river's current, animalcule in the eye of the tornado, in the space of five seconds he's snorted up, gulped down by the mall's swinging doors.

Where the air, being conditioned, makes him come to his senses. It's the time of day when the workforce is out to lunch, the hour for running little errands: no shortage of people, no shortage of women, and so no shortage of jumbled perfumes— the greens and the ambers, the vanillas and the musk, the great classics alongside the little discounts. While continuing forward, Meyer restarts his recognition game from earlier, but he subtly brakes when he finds himself in the wake of the one among them that he knows. Which he's already encountered. Of the five to six hundred thousand reactions that a perfume can have on someone's body, this one alone, once, Meyer has come across. He turns, looks around him.

The trail is coming from, it seems, a pack of people marching toward the big elevators. Meyer joins the pack, shoves his way through it, advances to the front. The strength of the perfume has dissipated but several encouraging molecules still manage to reach him, which he uses to guide himself, to take his bearings, following them like footprints: he charges into the three-quarters full elevator.

At the back of the elevator designed for thirty people, raised up onto the tips of his toes, bingo: he sees her. He's seen her. Mercedes. He can see her clearly. Meyer gets pushed. The elevator doors are about to close. And just then, at 12:50, the earth begins to shake. But it's very subtle, and no one notices.

9

IT SHAKES A THOUSAND OR SO times per day, let's not forget. Just about everywhere, though a little more often than average near the Mediterranean. Because beneath its easygoing and blue exterior, lemon-yellow, easygoing, green, the innocent Riviera serves as a cover to the subterranean battle being played out between the African and Eurasian continental plates. Below us Africa ceaselessly attacks, carrying out its assault, striving to annex three inches of ground from Eurasia, which normally concedes about fifteen millimeters per year. But sometimes Eurasia fights back, resists, refuses to go along with African extortion. A mistake: everyone loses because the faults immediately deteriorate, each party straining toward the point of rupture. And if the planets' alignment happens to be amplifying Earth's gravity, then the entire zone gives way and jolts, the entire foundation is at risk of rattling. Various warning signs, sometimes—showers of sand or blood, tension in the farmyards and on the freeways, out of season heat lightning—portend these phenomena, but most of the time the earth barely shakes at all and no one notices other than the dogs, nothing reacts besides the hypersensitive triggers of home alarm systems. Fortunately, it's quite rare that this discreet bump is followed by an aftershock. Fortunately.

And so, in the neighborhood surrounding Nicole's villa, three or four house alarms should've gone off at the same time, sirens more or less immediately shut off. Seeing no sign of danger, a large red hairbrush in hand, Nicole looks out over the carefree landscape: the white comings and goings of sails, seagulls against the two large dominant blue backgrounds, shimmering sun, hills of ochre and chalk, Mexichrome, natural colors and all rights reserved. A barely awakened Nicole is wearing nothing more than a large square of cloth, covered in big mauve and teal hydrangeas, tied in the front. Brushes unthinkingly, taking her time, collects the hairs left between the bristles then arranges them, on the edge of a geranium, for the birds who will use them to build their shelters—ideal reinforcement for their concrete, hair, a binder without equal for nest building. To the left of the carefree landscape, Nicole watches the apartment towers erected at the foot of the hills, the construction of a final tower on the right.

Two cranes stand over the site, one yellow with a red flag, one green with a green flag, turned toward each other in a duel. One after the other they bend toward the site like two eponymous wading birds drinking in turn from the same source of water before enjoying a long break when the ants below, turning to the services of an excavator mole or drilling earthworm, no longer need them. Bearing the company's initials, each flag is fixed astern the lifting apparatus, above the counterbalance of the jib, far behind the crane operator and his cabin, who sometimes gets bored during the breaks, between two transfers of material. Also at the crane operator's disposal is a little toolbox of diversions, a couple of things to help him get through the day: power-ful binoculars and a little radio stuck on Radio Monte Carlo, a walkie-talkie through which the boss of the ants gives his instructions, cans and snacks wrapped in the morning's paper. During these empty moments, through the walkie-talkies, the two crane operators exchange the worksite's labor-union gos-sip, displaying a fighter pilot's contempt for the ground crew. But the major interest of course is the entertainment from the nearby towers, all the things that can be seen through their windows, dozens of little screens gushing out soap operas, social documentaries, cooking shows, domestic sitcoms, and erotic series, which the crane workers especially enjoy bingeing on. Obligingly signaling one another, tower 4 floor 12 window 6, such a pleasant variety show of mating, the powerful binoculars suddenly become useful.

Nicole, just about nude on her terrace, was spotted immediately by the binoculars.

Leaning against the railing, Nicole dissects the soundtrack, identifies the noises one by one, near and far. Calls of melancholic seagulls, gargling of discount pigeons, chirping of sparrows with their tiny engines, hymenoptera buzzing in the mock orange. Line of a 747 en route toward a happier horizon, sizzling of traffic on the cliff road. Exclamations of some guy down the street helping another one to park his van. Then, behind her, Nicole hears the groan of a sink inside the villa, the click of an opening door, the jangling of the curtain that separates the terrace from the living room. Bill, I suppose. Nicole doesn't bother to turn around.

He comes up to her, he's as close as he could possibly be, his hands taking a stroll through the hydrangeas. With a minuscule sleight of hand, he's untied the piece of cloth and the flowers fall crumpled to the ground. In the distance the cranes come to a sudden halt, shouts of joy in the walkie-talkies greet the fall of the hydrangeas, the binoculars' focus wheels spin around on themselves at full speed, sprinting feverishly toward clarification. The excitement reaches an apogee in the cabins, which start searching for the best angle of observation, the motors growling in nervous fits and starts while Bill commences, him as well, to growl quietly behind Nicole. Then it seems that other deep growls can suddenly be heard—but where are they coming from?—growls much deeper than the others, and at that exact moment Nicole loses her balance before falling uncontrollably over. Behind her Bill also falls over, but slowly at first, just like the glasses sliding smoothly off the table, the ashtrays, the coffee cups, which then topple over and explode at their feet; and now everything seems to be shattering inside the villa, everything beginning to dance through the commotion. There it is, the aftershock, it's here, it's starting to shake again, but this time it's not fooling around.

During her slow motion fall, Nicole has the time to notice that the living room curtain is no longer plumb, then that the entire façade of the villa has begun to crack apart in rapid fissures, instantaneous, pens writing out the apocalypse at a demonic speed; beneath them the depths roar, increasingly violent thunder coming from the wrong direction. In the distance, throughout the entire city, a harmony of alarms has again been triggered, every imaginable variety of siren superimposed one on top of the other, blended: shrill trills, sour car-horn juice, repetitive and mournful wee wees, squealing cucarachas—spontaneous mutiny from the herd of automobiles, as unpredictable as an uprising of the calves.

Dodging the fall of a first beam, Bill, having not let go of Nicole, pulls her toward the terrace's stairs, which they then barrel down toward the street, distancing themselves from the ready-to-crumble villa, surrounded by quivering pine trees and sinusoid power poles nearing their breaking point. Reaching a small clearing at the edge of the road, an open air parking lot where there's no risk of anything falling from above, they throw themselves to the ground, cling desperately to the agitated earth without witnessing, not so far off in the distance, the cranes collapse into their worksite, without hearing the screams of terror that flood the walkie-talkies.

It was bright blue, the sky, but now it's completely white, a dull white more blinding than the invisible sun, a paleness streaked through with flashes, with long quicksilver tears, striped, furious, above a ground that is itself getting ripped apart, forking out into a thousand fissures as if two mirrors were exploding face to face. Beneath her, against her stomach, Nicole feels a shockwave plow through the depths, a huge panicked subterranean beast burrowing into its den, the contraction of an enormous, dilated intestine. Immediately afterward, the wave shakes the villa: breaking of windows and collective suicide of the dishes, a final slamming of doors before total destruction. The house jolts on itself, sits down again slightly askew, then the wave continues on its journey east, knocking over everything in its path, straight toward the towers lined up at the foot of the hills.

A first tower comes to pieces and then the others follow suit, one sinking into the ground up to its hilt while another, expulsed from the ground, blasts off before crumbling at an angle; the final three topple into one another like dominoes. And above the bass line of seismic roaring rise up choirs of screams, the voracious crackling of the first fires, the squawking of sirens and the counterpoint of clocks from the Major and Saint-Victor, from Réformés, from Notre-Dame-du-Mont-Carmel, a dead drunk jangling no longer in accordance with anything, Angelus or tocsin, muddling up vespers and matins before, one after another, following the spread of the wave, the bell towers overturn. And take note that since things have begun shaking, only nine seconds have gone by. Take note.

10

THEN REMIND YOURSELF THAT distress, terror, distorts our perception of time, that panic makes everything go slower. Imagine the atmosphere in the elevator. After the doors had closed, Meyer, with persistent staring, had finally managed to snatch a fleeting sign of recognition from Mercedes, an automatic nod of the head and a mechanical smile, the kind of forced politeness that also governs relations between slices of roast beef, without condiment, stacked inside a Tupperware box in the fridge. Meyer didn't insist. This all right after the elevator had started rising, indifferent to the first weak tremor, and right before the second came to kill its momentum, violently; that time, everything began to shake.

The whole mall had shuddered in the aftershock, from the mortar of the foundations to the finest nerve endings. Its well-balanced mass wouldn't suffer much serious damage, but the shock must still have broken certain circuits because the elevator immediately froze between two floors, thrown simultaneously into darkness. Silence. No doubt powered separately, only the Muzak persists at a low volume, an interior monologue of shapeless violins and sweating synthesizer.

After the brief sideration then the scattered exclamations, the simple questions, the flicking of lighters, several fingers hurry toward the red emergency button. Impressions are exchanged, everyone has heard the buzzing (according to some), the crunching (according to others) that preceded the elevator's stop. The some are persuaded that it's minor, a growing quantity of others very quickly begin to feel trapped, buried alive in a collective sarcophagus where time is becoming increasingly slower. For just a moment, near the flame of a Zippo, Meyer makes out the calm profile of Mercedes. A child cries behind him then a first woman seems on the verge of moaning, someone breaks into tears at the back right, a man just next to Meyer begins repeating softly, Gérard, Gérard, Gérard, Gérard, Gérard, it soon becomes unbearable and probably nothing would have been able to shut them all up if the third tremor, incomparable to its predecessors, wasn't then triggered.

Now, the whole city is going to shake. From the depths of the neighborhoods comes a variety of rackets, rumbling of crushed scrap iron beneath the Pomme, cyclopian infrasounds below the Rose, while in the entrails of the Merlan it seems as if a charge of tanks has been sent over cobblestone, all their artillery going off at once. Everywhere it creaks and cracks like when it's really about to move while the sky hicks up several arpeggios of sound barrier. And during the brief pauses in the roar of rombos, retumbos, bramidos, already the clamors of distress, the moaning and the screams of terror, can be heard rising up: no requiem without a solid choir section.

It'll be from the east, with brute force, that the shockwave will return, an enormous subterranean ripple sent straight through the city center, a living toboggan lifting up the green spaces and the avenues, the monuments, the buildings. Some of these buildings are quite old, their brass balls bouncing balero-like on their ancient banisters; when the wave has passed, these buildings sometimes fall to pieces. Sometimes entire blocks collapse in unison. Sometimes, held up by a neighbor, they remain standing at a tilt, bent over like a man vomiting off balance and likewise emptying themselves through every orifice of the objects and frantic people contained within. Newer buildings hold up better, although even the mall, constructed following earthquake-resistant standards, suffers serious nerve damage. Total short-circuit. Fractures to water inlets, to gas mains. Rupture of elevator cables: in a flash of weightlessness, accompanied by screams and invocations, names of gods pleaded to and taken in vain, the elevator is sucked into the blackness toward the center of the earth, its occupants tangling together during the endless fall.

Now it's shaking just about everywhere, the stairs at the train station wave like a sheet snapped through a window, its hundred steps stream into one another and erupt, a rapid washing away of stone heads and bronze trophies, groups of bouncing cherubs. The palm trees, on both sides, undulate more than they would've ever dared wish for while the city's lofty allegory, place Castellane, begins to crack longitudinally. A schism appears atop her crowned head, a sharp division that spreads downward and divides her forehead before severing her shoulders and breasts in half and separating the emblems nestled in her arms. It reaches the base of the column where the fountain begins convulsively spitting out a crimson liquid. Then buckling in on itself, the monument collapses, breaks to pieces over the banks and bars that surround the square.

Very soon, across the city, fleeing the domiciles that can no longer ensure protection from anything, quite a crowd finds itself out in the street beneath a hot rain of glass and concrete fragments, of metal debris, of freestone and flowerpots. At first they rush back into the houses, then come back out when it lets up a little. Blinded by the dust, people push in all directions until a majority seems to opt for the seaside. Scenes of crowds. People scramble and shove their way toward the harbor, they all have more or less the same expression though they're not all entirely dressed; some of them clutch some barely salvaged item against their body, something unpredictable, which could be a passport just as often as it's a fox terrier. Which could be a bag, a turntable, a parasol in its cover, a printout of computer code, a pocket edition of an Annabel Buffet novel. A burst of supplementary panic overcomes the crowd when the basilica top pops off, its rejected dome scattering over the social security of rue Jules-Moulet. Wide shots of the panicked crowd, medium shot of Cynthia running through the crowd: we see Cynthia pass in front of the number 68 tram, which has overturned on boulevard Chave, no sign of the stocky young man she left with last night. Reverse shot of the ocean, which in these circumstances is the embodiment of refuge, security. The ocean keeps its calm at the bedside of earthquakes, and then of course nothing is built on top of it, nothing can come smashing down over it, no risk of debris crushing your skull. Or so they believe, these poor, naïve people.

Several cracks have opened up to the east of the Vieux-Port, arborescent crevasses in the exact center of the street, some of them exuding a hot black material or maybe only hot black vapors. Whole colonies of insects rush out of them, a large reptile or two, it smells like chlorine and ether, sulfur and noble gases, there are already several rats running around nearby. If some of these fissures, no larger than a ditch, will remain gaping open after the disaster, other much wider ones are just as soon snapped shut, swallowing up men along with animals, squeezing them into a state of future fossils to be extracted, in five thousand years, for sums unheard of in their lifetime.

But for the moment, while Marseille goes on shaking, a whole section of its underwater basement, in the distance, begins to tilt. Abruptly, the bottom of the ocean floor has fallen. Naturally, this phenomenon provokes a violent displacement of water: and so now a wave appears on the horizon. Fleeing the city center and its murderous flowerpots, the first to arrive at the harbor immediately catch sight of it in the distance, this wave. It seems rather large. It also seems to be approaching rather quickly.

A wall as high as a large building, as deep as three buildings and as wide as two hundred, hurls toward the coast with the speed of a locomotive, tipping over and flinging high into the air every fishing barge and pleasure boat in its path. The Solange-IV

and the Marie-Martine flutter about, adieu Cephalonic, bye-
bye Double Nelson, the anchors at the end of their chains twirl
through the air, the hulls explode and the masts snap to pieces
before falling back shattered into the monster, which swallows
them forthwith. The tidal wave even dispatches a small oil
tanker, moving through the air at the peak of its crest, onto a
gas storage area before coming down on top of the harbor, crash-
ing over it and well beyond, submerging everything up until the
train station, coming to sprawl halfway up the pulverized stairs.
The stock of gas begins to burn, then the wave withdraws.

But it's not going to withdraw immediately: the monster prefers, first, to completely trample the adversary, to linger over its
prey, kicking the downed player and smothering it a little more
before finishing it off. Then the wave calmly retreats, the objects
formless and the bodies lifeless; it withdraws leisurely, takes its
time to reveal the extent of the damage, slowly, like someone
unveiling a sculpture or a lazy stripper undressing. Having
deeply excavated the coastal expanse, it leaves behind—on the
roofs, the balconies, the ledges—fish unknown even to the fish-
ermen, blind giants or dwarfs from a thousand meters below the
surface. There are even several catches of octopus piled up where
before only the seagulls had reigned, whose struck down bodies
now float, symmetrically, half-above and half-below the water's
surface. The surf bubbles for another moment, then silence sets
in until the arrival of the first rescue workers.

11

— FOLLOW ME, SAID MEYER.

At the end of its blind drop following the third tremor, the elevator had come to a violent halt at its point of departure, on floor 1. Two sexes, three generations, and four or five skin colors found themselves entangled inside the dark elevator, screaming out in fright as if on a scenic railway. After unknotting themselves, bumping into one another as they got back onto their feet, they began discussing the best way to get out.

Lacking power, the door stayed put instead of automatically opening; one of the first men back on his feet examined it in the flicker of his naphtha lighter. The blackish, foul-smelling flame was blurrily reflected in the brushed metal doors—separated by a strip of thick black rubber—which another man, owner of a pocket knife, simultaneously set about trying to force open. Introducing his blade into the slit, he began rummaging inside it as if trying to open an oyster. After the counterpoint of clamors that had accompanied the elevator's fall, a deep silence now reigned, a contemplation worthy of a dentist's office, everyone concentrated on the small scratching noise of the forceps. All eyes were on the man with the knife, crouched next to the man with the lighter.

Opinel and Zippo must have isolated then severed the appropriate muscle, the correct nerve, because with a light, muffled click the doors were released. But they didn't give way completely, didn't withdraw—only loosened, they offered just a thin opening through which a small amount of dark gray air smelling of burnt film passed. Immediately crowded near the door, men and several women had thrown themselves fiercely upon it, pulling from both sides as they swore and growled beneath their breath, forcing the doors to clear the way. As soon as they'd capitulated, Meyer watched Zippo, followed by Opinel, rush toward the exterior only to freeze near the threshold of the elevator, take a step back on a carpet of debris, then take off again more slowly into the darkness, cautious sleepwalkers.

Not a single living soul outside, not even a neon light. Without reflecting off the broken mirrors, blocks of light could be seen in the distance near the mall's exit, lighting the entrances of the deserted shops and allowing them to just barely find their way. The beginning of a fire, spontaneously extinguished, had taken hold of a nearby stand selling photography equipment, several red dots still ran along the unrolled strips of film. One after another they came out of the elevator, tripping at first over the mess of broken objects then moving away toward the dim light in the distance. Meyer, having been among the first to go through the door, chose not to follow the others and remained near the elevator, watching the exit. As soon as Mercedes appeared, he took her by the arm. Follow me, he said.

It wouldn't be much easier to see outside the mall: they now entered an extremely opaque cloud, extremely thick, one layer piled on top of another, a fusion of smoke, compact particles, and powdered concrete, breathable only by cockroaches, that concealed anything further than sixty centimeters away: they thought they were coming out into open air, they walked into a bag of cement. The survivors from the elevator pushed open the door then surged hastily back inside. Still holding onto Mercedes's arm, Meyer went back toward the first shops. Stepping into the shop displays, he swiped two pairs of sunglasses from a display rack, several scarves without taking the

time to choose specific colors, then wrapped his head like a
Bedouin, demonstrating to Mercedes how it's done. Then just
before leaving the mall, with a finger placed on his sternum,
he turned to her and said: Louis. A little smile, maybe, behind
the sunglasses, but no name from beneath the scarves. Fine, no
problem, we'll stick with Mercedes. Let's go.

But once outside, walking through the haze required so
much effort that it was like moving through a swamp. After
about fifty meters, while trying to make out his feet, Meyer
finally understood that it was, in fact, a swamp. As it'd retreated,
the giant wave had left in its wake a syrupy mud, a large sticky
mortar, supplemented with shards, that rose above your ankles
and still seemed to be moving, slowly, toward the newly estab-
lished sea level. Meyer moved forward, at first with no visual
markers, holding Mercedes firmly by the wrist. When he turned
toward her, barely able to make her out at the end of his arm,
he almost collided with an overturned car, its roof sunken into
the sludge up to its side-view mirrors, its muddy wheels pointing
up into the soot.

Since a goal was necessary, as usual, Meyer had decided to
move away from the ocean, not entirely certain of the sound-
ness of his choice, nor even entirely certain of going in the right
direction—not only is it impossible to see anything, he doesn't
know Marseille that well. He decided to orient himself using
the edge of a sidewalk at the bottom of the marsh, trying to
more or less follow this edge. The cloud soon seemed to dilute
a little, more and more overturned cars could be made out in
the surroundings, asphyxiated tortoises sometimes sitting one
on top of another, though they couldn't make out the presence
of anybody behind their filthy windows. Meyer and Mercedes
also noticed, more clearly, several buildings standing to their
left, several façades where balconies hung by a thread of wrought
iron. Isolated silhouettes took shape in the distance, small wandering groups just like the two of them but indistinct to the
point of seeming improbable, the idea of joining them didn't

even cross Meyer's mind. He moved forward while continuing to
guide Mercedes, still holding her though now by the hand, the
radio in his other; it seemed to him that they'd walked almost
an hour before coming out of the cloud by distancing themselves from the harbor. Then, at last, the sky was visible, still
extremely white and still crossed through with little flashes—but
dimmed, less blinding, even somewhat beautiful, from silver
toward yellow and mauve or pink, followed by crashes further
and further away in the distance. It felt like they could breathe
again. Removing his camel rider's mask, Meyer looked over the
extent of the damage.

Up to the level of Les Réformés, the entire lower half of
the city was still covered in dust and mud, sitting in the dazed
silence of a curfew, of a ceasefire. Heavy silence, chemical, post-
operative, worse than a Sunday and amplified by scattered cries,
groans, several calls for help but on the whole not as many as you
might expect. Slow, soundless shadows continued to float out
from the cloud, seeking the unscathed parts of town. From here,
the ocean was out of sight. What should we do? asked Meyer.
Since their escape from the elevator, they hadn't exchanged more
than six words. I think that you can let go of my hand now,
Mercedes replied. Sorry, right, said Meyer as he opened his fingers, but what are we going to do? We go back to Paris, said the
young woman while turning around. And already moving away.

Meyer was in complete agreement. But, quickening his pace
to reach her, he pointed out that the disaster must have dis-
rupted, big time, the public transport system, that it was thus
impossible to get away without a vehicle. Of his own car, surely
destroyed like the others, remained only the keys in his pocket
and the radio, still here, covered in marks at the end of his arm, I
don't even know why I still have it. In the absence of a response,
they continued walking north.

Putting further distance between themselves and the earthquake's epicenter, they soon came to intact neighborhoods.
Meyer heard, from far off, the first emergency vehicles. In a

shopping street before Saint-Barnabé, a fair amount of people had come out from shops, from offices, from bars, had stopped on the sidewalks, a fair amount of people were looking out their windows, all of them watching the same spot on the horizon. Low volume commentary between friends and family or to one-self alone, no one looking at anyone else, everyone watching the spot as if it were a hearse. The street ended in an equilat-eral square, a quarter of which contained a public garden and a fountain; to the left a large Total garage and General Motors dealership, to the right a café terrace. As they walked along the garden, the fountain began to blush, cough, blacken while suf-focating on misplaced remarks from its siphon, finally drying up with the groan of a bus door. I'm thirsty, said Mercedes.

She hadn't voiced a single thought until then, hadn't opened up in the least, crossing the disaster without a word of com-mentary, face unreadable, as distant and detached as she was on the freeway while speaking into the phone beside her burning car, the day before. The day before? Meyer repeated to himself. Let's see. Let's do a recap. Oh yes, yesterday. Strange. It seemed longer. Me too, he said, I'm kind of thirsty.

The young woman chose an armchair at the end of the ter-race, near a plane tree. A waiter walked up unhurriedly with his eyes on the sky, which was crossed through with a brown col-umn above the gas storage area, in the distance. Mercedes asked for mineral water and if it'd be possible to use the telephone, then went into the bar from which escaped staticky pop music.

— A dry white, decided Meyer.

The waiter lingered for a moment, continuing to look off into the distance, while Meyer examined the swollen initials and cicatricial hearts carved into the plane tree's trunk: as if onto a sick body, infused, bandaged, mimeographed notes and manuscripts were taped directly to the bark, tacked into the living wood, in search of cleaning hours or a lost red dog, bus schedules or the performance of a local rock and roll band, next Thursday, live at the community event center. Mercedes soon reappeared, lamenting the petrochemical taste of the mineral water and the out of order of telephone: definitely overloaded, possibly damaged, the network was refusing all calls to Paris. Then, having extracted a small mirror from her handbag and glancing into it as if at a stranger, the sharp clacking of its clasp must have been the signal for departure: Meyer looked through his pockets for money.

As he entered the bar to pay, the pop songs were interrupted, dispelled by the gong of a newsflash. Marseille, said an urgent voice, significant earthquake. The gravity of the situation has yet to be properly assessed but the figures, already, look devastating. A first summary in our four o'clock newscast, but at this very moment I'm calling our permanent onsite correspondent. Meyer pocketed his change. Yes, Jean-Luc, indeed, I'm presently at cours Belsunce and what I'm looking at cannot be described. You cannot describe it. You simply cannot. However, I'm going to try.

Without waiting, Mercedes had started toward the Total garage while radios, awakened by the newsflash and playing at maximum volume, overlapped each other through the open windows, escaped in every direction from the apartments, the caustic telephones making oblique saw cuts through the air. Meyer, in turn, crossed the square. Although their pipes were fastened to the pumps and the clinking of tools could be heard from the workshop, the garage seemed closed. The young woman stopped in front of the large showroom window to study the sales models, beef-blood sedan, straw-colored station wagon, little yellow convertible coupé with automatic transmission. So many cars, so many life choices, Meyer thought to himself, what's she going to take?

To the very brown man in the glass booth, androgenic hair squeezed beneath overalls open to his plexus, completely black hands wiped with an even blacker rag, Mercedes announced that she wished to buy one of these cars while the radio on the desk continued the report from our onsite permanent correspondent:

the first rescue efforts were being organized to deal with a situation, Jean-Luc, which is, I remind you, still extremely unclear. Which one, asked the man as he lowered the volume. The little yellow one, said the young woman. Remaining very calm on the outside, on the inside Meyer felt a rush of excitement, smiling perhaps a little too much when Mercedes handed him the keys. Check signed, doors slammed, he slid the radio into its compartment beneath the ashtray, then seconds later the topless coupe was heading north through the suburbs.

Meyer wanted to get on the freeway as soon as possible but, to begin with, he didn't know where to find an onramp, and then the four o'clock newscast informed him that this was impossible: the freeway had suffered serious damage, two-thirds of its suspended section had collapsed. The tunnel that ran below the harbor had succumbed as well, split into pieces then flooded with water. Further north, beyond the train station, the freeway's surface undulated in a succession of arcs, which became increasingly steep toward the epicenter—those closest had even burst open, broken by the shockwave; their interiors were thus on display, offering a sectional view of their strata of sand, of concrete, of porous asphalt and asphalt concrete. All circulation being impossible before the Aix-en-Provence junction, Meyer did a lengthy improvisation on a series of back roads, once again the suburbs, the countryside—tall trees and yellow houses, cultivated acres, orchards. The quickly returning nature seemed unaware of the earthquake, a stranger to the disaster. You would've thought nothing had happened if not for the onsite correspondent giving a precise account of the rescue efforts, the help from the Red Cross, the recourse to the army, the deployment of the Orsec plan and the rumors of spontaneously organized gangs of looters. The event was on every national station, and the stations in nearby countries also had nothing else to talk about; Meyer ended up switching off the radio.

12

KNOWING THE SKY AS WELL as I do, I should have suspected that things were taking a turn for the worse. Those hideous red blotches toward the south since the beginning of the week, scattered irritations on an unusually pale backdrop, didn't bode well at all. Then it happened, the earth shook, on every station there was nothing else being talked about. I switched off the TV.

I went back out to the terrace, inspected the heavens, the sky was showing healthy colors again, I went back in. Just to amuse myself a little I woke up Titov, who opened one innocent eye, a second inquiring eye, surely not too happy about having his sleep interrupted but taking care to hide his feelings. Sweet creature. I signaled to him to move around a little and pointed to the French window. He shook himself off, lifted his shoulders, then crossed the threshold of his room. I took in his scent as he passed in front of me, slowly, with the boldly resigned attitude of someone leaving for work. Suddenly, I became irritated with him. As I motioned for him to pick up the pace, he made another movement, without turning around, that seemed to say I'm going, I'm going. I watched him embark onto the terrace from where he would've had no trouble reaching the neighboring roofs. But I wasn't worried. I know my Titov, he wouldn't run away. At the edge of the terrace I watched him bend over toward the street then lift his eyes toward the sky and take a deep breath. Blinking his eyes. Shaking his head. Sniffing a little. Titov. My irritation suddenly evaporated, and I was overcome by affection: all right, come in, I told him, go back to sleep. I didn't have to say it twice.

Afterward I called Lucie at her office. Still not here, her secretary told me. Too bad. I would've found a way, casually, to let my feelings be known. Have you heard from Blondel? I would've asked for example. It seems that things have been set into motion, she would've answered, he seems a little worked up to me. Nothing's signed yet but he wants us to be ready. For you, Lucie, I would've then said profoundly, I will always be ready— although I'd try to proceed a little more shrewdly, more allusively, less head on. You make me laugh, she would've laughed all the same, you know quite well that I'm a very watched over woman. Besides, I think there's someone ringing your doorbell.

Indeed, though I hadn't been expecting anybody, the bell was ringing. I'm going to let you go, Lucie would've said, it must be one of your lady friends. I would've protested, would've heard her smile before hanging up. I went to the door: Max. You could've called ahead, I said.

Max had trimmed his beard again. The better things go for him, the less he hides behind it. Milan, Cologne, Houston, Tokyo: each exhibition of some importance makes him go one notch closer with his clippers. He was bringing me the catalogue of his retrospective in Oslo, happy for having sold every piece on display at Pontarlier's to the Japanese man. Even me? I asked. Yes. Even you. A big insurance agent from Osaka. And what's new with you? Still on work leave? Hopefully not for much longer, I replied. It looks like things are coming together. What'll you have to drink?

With Max gone, I get back aboard the home trainer. Abdominals, abdominals, then Jacqueline comes by around five o'clock, as planned. As usual she puts her purse on the armchair then goes to sit on the divan. I bring her a cup of tea, I sit down next to her and take her into my arms.

But my heart's not entirely into it, I know that Blondel will be calling shortly. At the least appropriate moment no doubt. I can already see how it's going to unfold. He's going to want to tell me about his latest idea. He's going to ask me if I remember, for example, Senator E. J. Garn? on Discovery? in April 1985? Not really, I'll respond. They'd thrust him into being specialist of payload, he'll remind me. You can imagine what that meant for the poor guy. Guinea pig for all the biomedical and paramedical. Okay, I'll say, and so? So we're going to do the same with the civilian. Great, I'll say, that's a great idea. I'm not the one who should be congratulated, he'll say modestly, it's Vuarcheix that came up with the idea. By the way, you haven't forgotten to prepare for the broadcast over Hawaii, have you? Did you come up with anything? I've got a little something I've been running through my head, I'll respond, a little idea for a performance. Then I'll explain my little script to him. Really good, he'll enthuse, really really good. The idea with the string instruments is really very good.

And so it goes. Fifteen minutes later, Jacqueline and I are lying down, very much at it, very heated up. Then right as I'm getting ready to penetrate her: ringing of the telephone. I pick up immediately.

13

SILENCE IN THE LEMON-YELLOW coupe. Meyer had again tried, two or three times, to engage in conversation; Mercedes still wouldn't go along with him.

Just a deterrent noise of agreement, always the same two dead-end syllables: the kind of girl who stays quiet when you leave a movie. The type who finds it somewhat unrefined to comment on films without reflection, especially disaster movies, which she also happens to find terribly unrefined. Meyer eventually gave up. Back on the freeway after the Étang de Berre, they soon crossed paths with the reinforcements, a slow moving column of military vehicles, high beams in broad daylight, surrounded by jeeps with long, curving antennas. Then, toward Montélimar, the sky had clouded over. When it began raining—Meyer having stopped the coupe to put up the roof—the to and fro of the windshield wipers monopolized all sound and he began to feel as if time was dragging by. No middle ground in this man's life, it's either total thrills or total boredom

Hang in there, look out at the landscape, count the kilometers covered, the kilometers to come. Go through the list of the two hundred and fifty beds where Meyer's slept, draw up afterward that of the women he's been with, now calculate the intersection of these two sets; more complicated than it might sound. Read the license plates of passing cars. Worry about his own car, wonder about the car's insurance, about the existence or not of a natural disasters clause in the contract. Worry about Nicole and Marion, about Cynthia, about Élizabeth Frise and her quantity surveyor at the heart of the natural disaster. Scold himself for having worried about his car first.

Turning all this over in his head, Meyer threw occasional sideways glances at Mercedes, sitting straight up and looking straight ahead as the freeway unfolded before her. On two occasions he saw her lips slightly tremble, a barely perceptible swell caused by the gust of a thought, a sirocco of an idea. Near Valence she seemed to be looking for something in her purse, or perhaps just taking an inventory: objects designed either to direct the course of things—canister of tear gas, birth control pills—or the appearance of things—lipstick, sunglasses, gloss. Always a little disconcerted, Meyer, when he sees pills in the purse of a stranger. Bashful as a young man. And to prove it, he's going to be a complete disgrace when Mercedes, finally, speaks to him. Without warning.

When she at last decides to say something:

— Did you see the horse at the back of that field over there?

Starting with a subject like this, obviously, the associations abound, the possible responses are endless. You already have the horse's beauty, the horse's majesty and loyalty, you have everything involving a horse in the movies, in paintings, in sculpture and architecture, you have races, you have circuses, wars, farms and horse butchers, you immediately have an abundance of possibilities and you can quickly find lots of others, a horse is truly the ideal point of departure for a conversation, the surefire opening line.

But, during the time required to understand this however simple sentence, the time required to find the animal in the landscape, a disconcerted Meyer, caught off guard, proves himself to be pathetic. Perhaps overwhelmed by the very quantity itself of possible responses, he rapidly tries to find one, he rapidly tries to find one. And finally hears himself say, oh yeah, the horse. The black horse. But it's a little too late and Mercedes has nothing more to say. Disappointed, Meyer. And when he finally comes up with an idea to tell the story about how he fell off a horse around fifteen-sixteen, the only time he'd ever mounted one, it's far too late, the black horse is too far behind and to be honest it's a pointless story, not to mention that it's a bad memory. Unhappy with himself, he puts an end to the agonized death cries of the windshield wipers, which have been groaning for how long, by the way, on the completely dry windshield.

Backups, traffic jams began to appear around Vienne, while in the opposite direction another flood of brand new military trucks streamed past with no sign of abatement, newly hatched from the assembly lines with fresh batches of conscripts inside. Then the traffic coagulates into a massive moronic bottleneck, resigned, frozen sauce in the open countryside, sometimes subjected to brief fits and starts, twitches of three or four meters. It's annoying but it might be another chance to talk, to have a little social success: Meyer pointed out that things weren't moving, that things weren't moving at all, and what time is it by the way.

He knows the way well, he also said. When they were leaving Marseille, he thought they'd get to Paris sometime around midnight. Now it's almost seven, there's barely an hour left of light, what should we do. I think I'm a little tired, Mercedes replies. And maybe I'm a little hungry too. She says this gently.

Meyer, now, should be delighted when the young woman, supposedly cold and closed off, proposes, just as gently, to get off the freeway as soon as possible and find a place to eat, maybe to sleep as well. Meyer should be happy. Meyer should find life warmer, more accommodating. He should find it more easygoing instead of letting himself get worked up and feverishly reciting to himself his fall from the horse, wondering if it's really worth taking the time to tell the story. Though even if I save it, the story, it's no real solution, it won't last an entire dinner. No question about it, Meyer is very intimidated. But I'm not panicking. We're not there yet. We haven't even reached the exit. There's no rush. We're still only moving several meters at a time. Leaving the freeway at the next off ramp, they then wandered ten kilometers before reaching a semi-rural town by the name of Eyzin-Pinet, a small cushy village tucked away from the traffic at the edge of a departmental veinlet, far from the congested arterials, far from the thromboses. Night fallen, deserted streets at dinnertime, though not so many lights on in the windows. Four young people on mopeds, a blue tractor, then the Hotel Negro-Welcome at the exit of Eyzin-Pinet. Meyer had never looked for a hotel room in the company of a woman under such conditions. It was twenty-five minutes to eight.

Open, the Hotel Negro-Welcome was empty. On both sides of a yellow-toothed keyboard, the hotelkeeper's bright farmer's cheekbones suggested either dry alcohol or crisp air or both. She wiped her large bony hands in an apron before handing them the keys of two non-adjacent rooms, Meyer's room smaller than the other but equipped with an unplugged black-and-white television set, sitting on the ground, the screen turned toward the wallpaper. They would eat at half past eight.

Meyer plugged in then turned around the TV, which took a minute to warm up, to try and remember how exactly it functioned, crackling and giving off a smell of dust and grilled spiders. Then he went to wash his hands. A bar of aggressively rose-scented soap, an extra-long rinsing to remove this supplementary smell; as he washed his fingers one by one, looking over his face with resignation, the mirror above the sink suddenly seemed to burst into flames.

Dazzled: every inch of Meyer's epidermis is drenched in icy sweat, a cold dirty water fills and flows through his veins. His strength abandons him completely, runs off whimpering in every direction, disappearing into the distance. Vertigo: folded in two, his heart gone MIA, his hands hooked around the slippery edge of the sink, Meyer falls heavily to his knees—his eyebrow colliding violently, on the way down, with the porcelain.

Grumbling, blaspheming beneath his breath, complaining as if there were someone there to listen, he crawls toward the bed, collapses on top of it, then gets back up to turn off the faucet before taking a towel and sitting back down, bent over, pressing the moist cloth to his eyebrow, continuing to swear but grumbling less. Gradually, after several minutes, his sheepish strength begins to return, awkwardly apologizing for its betrayal, well, its defection, retaking its place but avoiding any and all eye contact, clearly embarrassed. Now, now, says Meyer, it's nothing. Let's check the news.

The television seemed to have lost its own instruction manual: in sporadic waves, a line of static twisted the newscaster's face, while he also seemed to be suffering from a strong electronic bronchitis. His forehead waltzes from the shape of an arrow to that of an arch, although given the gravity of the news one didn't have the heart to make jokes. Sorrowful eyes below his eight furrowed eyebrows, the journalist went to the special correspondent, also indistinct on a background of what were likely ambulance lights, then to the staff scientist. It must be said that the entire Mediterranean basin is under permanent threat of earthquakes, Jean-Luc. This is certainly not the first time something like this has happened.

Meyer watched the news until dinnertime then threw his jacket back on and stood before the mirror, joylessly looking over himself. At the top right of his pale face, an already rapidly expanding bump would no doubt be turning Prussian blue before dessert, just what we need right now. Lots of problems for just one day, Meyer is exhausted. It feels like he's been through a lot.

Twenty-five past eight, he went down the stairs into the oversized dining room, not so well lit, but all for the better. Empty at the moment. Meyer chose, backed into a corner, the table where his bump would cast the smallest shadow. Through a half-open door in the distance, in another corner, came the engine-like sound of a calm conversation between four people, or three people accompanied by a dog, in a block of complete ambient silence. It's the countryside, Meyer reminded himself while looking over the menu, it's exotic and reassuring the first day, sometimes even the second. Then he smiled clumsily as he lifted himself up, also clumsily. There she is.

The young woman had made better use of the bathroom than he had, clean and fresh but without any makeup, as if to highlight the limited purpose for having washed up: for herself alone, and not for the eyes of anyone else. She closed her barely consulted menu, immediately sure of her choice while Meyer still had very large doubts regarding the subject. But since out of the darkness, at the end of the table, a midget waitress had just materialized, Meyer, exhausted by his doubts, let Mercedes order and then took the same thing, let's say escalope with crudités, a carafe of water for her, a quarter-liter of wine for him, yes. The dwarf dissolved, Mercedes unfolded her napkin. Were you able to rest a bit? Meyer tried bravely. Mercedes looked up at him, her eyes immediately landing on the spot above his right eye.

— Yeah, grimaced Meyer while delicately touching the eyebrow, I banged myself up a bit. Nothing too bad though.

He wasn't expecting the young woman to then reach a hand out toward his face and, with the tips of her fingers, gently explore the area surrounding the bruise: and how did you do it?

— I'm just a little exhausted, he replied modestly. A little dizzy spell. It happens from time to time.

Not often. No more than two or three times a year. Usually in the morning, it seemed. Usually Sunday morning it seemed to him, but he refrained from specifying. You're going to have a hell of a bump, Mercedes smiled as she drew back her hand. Really kind sometimes, this girl, and then nothing more. Meyer returned the smile, but afterward found no way to draw out anything else. He'd of course try again, during the meal, to talk a little, but she would remain imprecise, politely evasive, vague: Meyer's risky topics of conversation, his questions, his attempts at engagement would all shatter without a response against the

opposing wall before plummeting weakly to the ground. A fes-
tive evening.

Nothing too exciting behind the half-open door either, at the
other end of the dining room: things were no longer going so
well between the three or four people and the dog. Some wine?
asked Meyer. Thanks, declined the young woman as she poured
herself a glass of water. Never had such bad tap water, she then
remarked while gently pushing away, with the tip of her pointed
shoe, the deflated questions scattered about her feet.

At this rate, no point in dawdling about, dessert quickly
disposed of, skip the coffee. Back up in his room, Meyer turns
on the TV again. It seems to be some kind of variety show, but
neither the image nor the sound is coming in right. Beneath a
static wave swelling his jaw into a wineskin and carving his ears
to a point, it's not without difficulty that the clown explains
that, despite the drama in Marseille, which affects us all, the
show must go on.

14

— THE FULL, SAID MEYER.

Each party back in their bedroom after the continental breakfast, a quick stop at the Eyzin-Pinet newsagent, then the yellow coupe pulls out of the gas station. Back on the freeway. Mercedes is deep into the dailies, no interest in either Meyer or the surroundings. The surroundings are flat, unexciting, everything the same shade of green, they get the attention they deserve, no reason to be offended. Meyer, on the other hand, who is offended, hears himself ask the young woman in a somewhat tense voice, too curt but too late, if she wouldn't mind summarizing the news for him.

According to her summary the earthquake, a 7.9 on the Richter scale, has obliterated Marseille's western port and three or four kilometers of the coastline; the epicenter is believed to be in the Liguria Sea. After the destructive impact of the two most powerful tremors, neither the fires nor the floods failed to do their part before the tidal wave came along to complete the disaster—a large number of victims, therefore, including a large proportion of cardiac arrests. According to rumors, gangs of looters formed immediately: through the open cracks in the Baumettes prison, groups of outlaws sentenced for life have escaped to plunder the jewelry shops, the gunsmiths, to rob the cadavers and the luxury groceries, to tear off earrings from the living and the dead, end of rumors. Next comes the extent of the fires and the details of the rescue efforts, the reactions of public figures, the historical precedents, a two-page spread by the staff scientist, should I move on? Yes, says Meyer, move on.

The coupe drives extremely well, almost on its own, overtaking a good number of other cars, sometimes even other coupes, Mercedes decides here to break off her summary. She reopens one of the dailies, takes a sly look at the horoscope section, Meyer doesn't dare ask her to read his own. He's mistaken. He should. In the renewed silence, his feet and fists at the controls and with no effort required to change gears on inclines, he advances. They're advancing. Sooner than expected it's the final stretch home, the last toll booth before Fontainebleau, Paris is no more than a quick missile blast away: as traffic speeds up and everyone's sprinting to be the first one to the big city, an impatient Meyer falls in with the momentum. After arriving he'll find it easier to breathe, once inside the peripheral he'll be more familiar with the names of things: in the enclosure bound by this highway, Meyer knows at any moment, always, where he is.

But not where he's going: as soon as they've past the porte d'Italie, he turns toward the young woman and asks again, so, what do we do? Half smiling, she gives an address, if it's not too much trouble, in the XVIth arrondissement. Perfect. Meyer knows the way.

With the car parked in front of an even number on the rue Cortambert, he inquiringly turns toward the young woman before she gets out, ready to ask her if they can see each other again. He's going to ask her the question. But since she's looking elsewhere, as if waiting for something, he realizes that he's the one who's supposed to get out. It doesn't take long to get used to a car, doesn't take long at all to develop a kind of intimacy with them, certainly doesn't take long at all for you to forget that they don't belong to you. Frustrated, Meyer, destabilized. Well, I'll leave you here, he says, forgetting to ask his question. Mechanically turning around to take his luggage he remembers now that he doesn't have any, that she doesn't have any either, that they're survivors with nothing on them, belched out unscathed from a disaster. See you later, he concludes, tripping as he opens the door. He nearly falls to the sidewalk, just barely catches himself on the lowered window, moves off without turning back. Doesn't remember until then that his radio's still in the car, quickly turns back but the yellow coupe, at first concealed by a very large van, Transports Sylvain Honhon, Lagny (S&M), has now disappeared. Not that important. The radio, Meyer won't be needing it for a while. And then there's always insurance. And then there could be a silver lining, maybe she'll want to return it to me, maybe she's going to come looking for me, maybe she's going to find me. One can always dream.

Back from the catastrophe, all alone on rue Cortambert with nothing on him but his dirty summer suit, Meyer spends yet another instant frozen on the sidewalk then follows it to the crossing at rue de la Tour. To the right again, then he crosses at the light, without hesitation, appearing very determined, evidently he knows where he's going. Then to the left at rue Desbordes-Valmore and there it is: a little affected building, dated, signed, moldings and wrought iron, a four-story wedding cake. Meyer types in the entry code, passes through the gate, presses a button on the intercom at the entrance, waits while watching a young woman dressed in cycling shorts and a shrug go by, a young work of art on high heels, in the streets women take the place of sculptures. What the hell is she doing in there, he says quietly while pushing the button again. Yes, a voice comes sighing at last, yes, the voice of a worried, languid, done-up woman. Mom, he says, it's me. The staircase smells principally of polish, a little bit like incense paper, a very little bit like mold.

My Lord, cries out Maguy Meyer, your shoes. Have you seen the state of your pants? I was in the countryside, Meyer improvises after they've hugged. A little mud, nothing serious. But look at you, he says, you're wearing that thing. You know, she says, that it reminds me of the captain.

The thing is a string of marcasites seasoned with zircons, winding through the collar of a big black sweater, accompanied by a black skirt and a black ribbon in a white bun, half-mourning. And the captain, who had already won a small role as sub-lieutenant during the bombing of Sakiet-Sidi-Youssef, aboard a French B-26 built by the Americans, 8 February 1958 (69 civilians killed, 130 injured), was the man who'd found himself promoted afterward to the top of the bill in Maguy Meyer's life. Who takes her son by the shoulders, look at me, you don't seem well. You've banged into something. Have you seen what you've done to yourself? Come, I'll put some Synthol on it. It's fine, says Meyer, I feel wonderful. But your eyes seem a little shiny. It's the country, he says, the air. On the other hand, do you mind if I take a bath?

You don't wear pants that have been dirtied up this bad. At the back of a bureau, Maguy looks for an alternative pair. Finds nothing in her son's size except a pair of jeans and a sweatshirt stiffened with paint, matching sneakers, from the time he came by to redo her entryway then stayed for dinner. Which doesn't happen anymore because his work takes up all his time. Now, from the bottom of the bathtub, Louis inspects the squadrons of cosmetics concentrated at the borders of the sink. His mother asks him, through the half-open door, questions, which he takes his time responding to, and at a reduced volume. And are you alone at the moment? she asks for example. I'm fine, he responds, I'm fine. That short one was so nice, Maguy recalls, and rather beautiful if you ask me. Maybe you should've stayed with her, don't you think? I know, sighs Meyer lazily, turning around as if in a bed, pulling a blanket of warm water over his shoulder, but we didn't have the same interests. Maguy closes the bureau. And did you see what happened in Marseille, she says while opening a closet, did you see how dreadful it is. Yes, says Meyer, it's terrible. At the back of the closet, at last, a pair of Robert Meyer's large bright tweed pants sits collecting dust, but Louis surely won't want to wear those. Maguy unfolds them anyway while raising her eyes to the sky, shaking her head and whispering to herself. Not the same interests.

Wrapped in a terrycloth towel, Louis, as predicted, refuses this alternative. No, I'll just put my old things back on, he says, I'll change back at my place. I should get back to my place. Which he says so miserably, maybe, that Maguy offers to go buy him something that he could put on now—as it happens there's a rather nice little men's store on rue de la Pompe. That's kind of you, says Meyer, but no. I haven't given you anything this year, Maguy reminds him, how about something dark for once. No, resists Meyer, no. Flannel in dark teal, something classic that would look nice on you. No, Meyer gives in, or maybe something black.

He's put his old things back on, his mother's gotten her purse, he joins her in the entryway. All right, he says, let's go? With a glance, Maguy makes a sign for him to move forward. If you think I'm going to be the one to open this door, she says, then we're not going anywhere.

15

BLACK GETS MARKED UP EASILY, that's the only real problem. But otherwise, the suit looked very good on Meyer. And so arm in arm, dressed in the same color, they went slowly back up rue de la Tour as if following, at a distance, an excessively fast funeral procession, already around the next corner. Then after having a salad, rue Desbordes-Valmore: sweetheart, Maguy says, don't you think we should go see him? We haven't been since last fall, don't you think we should go see him? All right, says Meyer, who thinks it's good to group related tasks together: came to visit his mother this morning, might as well stop by and see his father in the same stride, that way it's all taken care of in a single day.

Or at least stop by to see who's claimed to be Robert Meyer, beneath a stele engraved with the phrase *A British Airman of World War II—Known unto God*. Though not absolutely sure, Maguy's research has given her reason to believe that he's here, near the entrance of the military cemetery in the department of Aisne, not far from Charly-sur-Marne. A deserted cemetery in the glabrous countryside, two thousand identical monoliths topped with the same model of crescent, star, or cross, nothing above certain African names, not even a flower. At the back of the necropolis, two concrete containers harbor two collections—one with a hundred and thirty, the other two hundred and thirty—of unidentified bodies.

For ten minutes, a dry wind beneath an overcast sky beat

against the folds of their black outfits. Meyer, standing up very
straight, watched his bent over mother dust the monolith and set
two pieces of gravel on top of it, one black and one white, a sign
that they'd stopped by, then they'd started back toward Paris
in Maguy's Opel, on the same small roads that they'd come in
by. As usual Maguy, driving a little too fast, briefly evoked the
memory of Robert Meyer, whom Louis had practically never
known. Whom Maguy, moreover, had also barely known. No
remarkable feat, always the same three anecdotes; it was somewhat embarrassing that they were so much less interesting than
those that concerned the captain. And so, as they passed by an
old-fashioned inn at the edge of the Retz forest: I came here two
times with the captain, said Maguy. Can you imagine? Both
times, the first thing he did was set his revolver on the nightstand. Of course, that's another story.

She dropped off Meyer at the impasse of Morocco, call me,
kisses, you know you're handsome in that handsome suit of
yours. Then while he was looking for his keys in his new pockets, the telephone began ringing inside, just like the other time.
Shutters closed, current off, Meyer walked through the darkness
toward the phone. Absolutely not Victoria, that's for sure. No,
it's Blondel on the line again.

— Yeah, said Meyer, hello. Very good. Not at all, it's only
that I've just gotten back, wait. One second. Okay.

Blondel began to speak, Meyer to move about without really
listening—followed by the line tangling into knots throughout
the apartment—pushing open a shutter with one hand, opening
the current with another, gathering then briefly sorting through
the mail slid beneath his door: the bank, the gas bill, a postcard,
which he spun between his fingers, aerial view of Chicago with
the words Clear skies over Chicago. You can go to hell. Jo. It
is absolutely necessary that we see each other very soon, said
Blondel. Tomorrow morning a quarter past ten.

Afterward Meyer opened all the shutters then turned on the
radio: a solo piano, just what we need. Then he lowered himself

onto the big checkerboard couch and immediately stood back
up, relieved to finally be back, to find, after everything that had
happened, his quiet tidy home, thanking the heavens to have
escaped with his life. For several seconds—halfway between a
state of thankfulness and drunkenness—a feeling of overwhelm-
ing, slightly fanatic gratitude even made him look at worldly
things with a brand new, completely fresh interest: pissing then
flushing seemed like two astonishing miracles of nature and
technology. After which Meyer calmed down a bit, went to the
kitchen and prepared a tea. Cozy and dry, an extremely small
insect had set up shelter on one side of the kitchen sink, in the
reassuring shadow of the faucet, a friendly totem with its blue
eye, its red eye, and its long dripping nose. Now here came a
monstrous claw twisting the red eye, here came a scorching
whirlpool gushing out of the nose, a burning steaming spiral in
which the insect found himself immediately poached, heated
and reheated then, after six victory laps, sucked down the drain.
The day before, in a comparable heat, Meyer had been similarly
absorbed into the mall, toward the elevator, toward Mercedes,
who'd kept the radio, whose real name he didn't even know. He
served himself some tea, filled the ice tray.

Three hours later with his mind on a drink, the water in the
tray now frozen, Meyer removed the ice cubes. Adopt me, adopt
me—the ice cubes jumped joyously in their rubber molding, one
of them even flew up and settled into the fold of Meyer's naked
elbow. Very affectionate, this ice cube, he's obviously in search
of a master; Meyer adopted it into his glass, nice and warm in
the gin and tonic. Then he opened a box and made pasta. Spent
some time in front of the television: ice skaters going in reverse,
nothing he enjoys more, followed by wrestling, headlock while
twisting the head then crushing the head in a hold, sidestep and
a hit with the knee. Come midnight, Meyer, sunken deep into
his couch, made a last minute call to Georges, a very old friend,
one of those old friends to whom you've already told everything,
at least everything superfluous, only the essentials remain to be

discussed, and so what did you have to eat today.

The next morning, the sky's cloudy again and the telephone's ringing. Must be Blondel again. Absolutely not, it's Victoria.

16

I WON'T TAKE UP TOO MUCH of your time, said Victoria as she began to speak at great length, giving him a wholesale update of her life as if the past two years had meant nothing. Remarried with a sound engineer, living in the western suburbs over which, by the way, it should soon be raining. Still very interested in the weather, just like before, still very good at meteorology. She spoke fast, Meyer didn't catch everything. And so, she said, what about you?

Caught off guard and for lack of anything better, Meyer would try to summarize some of his projects at work and his related occupational activities, simplifying his research a little, embellishing the results, though Victoria wouldn't seem to totally follow the subject. Noise behind her at the other end of the line. Ah, she said, here's my husband. Characteristic husband noises followed, the sound of a wet kiss from a drenched husband returning home. You wouldn't believe how hard it's coming down, said Victoria. And all my love et cetera. If it was just for that, Meyer, had he the choice, would've preferred she hadn't called.

Tomorrow morning a quarter past ten, as Blondel had planned, and here we are. An old pink polo shirt beneath the brand new black suit resulted in something not too bad at all, even if Meyer post-Victoria's call wasn't feeling entirely himself—and Blondel not so bad either in an apple green jacket, which noticeably shed off the years. Through the windows of his office, rue de Varenne, it was still gray. On the sidewalk across the street, beneath the entrance of a private high school, three extra-light blondes were puffing on English cigarettes while waiting for something better to come along. I wasn't sure I'd be able to get a hold of you, yesterday, on the phone, said Blondel. I'd forgotten the dates of your vacation. Yeah, said Meyer, I had to cut it short. What, said Blondel, it didn't go so well, your vacation? What's that, did you hurt yourself? It's nothing, said Meyer, and it went extremely well. Perfect. You had good weather, ventured Blondel.

It was fine.

Still not really in the mood to talk about the disaster, no more to him than to Maguy. But Blondel pushed out his lips while waving a hand out in front of himself, as if he was giving a running commentary on a particularly violent boxing match. And so, he said, did you see what happened to Marseille? I did, said Meyer. You can't imagine the effect it's had, exclaimed Blondel. A little, said Meyer, I can imagine it a little.

— I mean to the ministry, the other specified. I mean for us. Would you believe they've granted the funding, for Sismo. It seems that we're back in business.

— Congratulations, said Meyer.

— The Sismo satellite, repeated Blondel, don't you remember? We've improved it, look. We found a solution.

He went off crabwise toward the wall safe behind his desk, dipping a hand into a coat pocket, from the inside of which he pressed three contacts on a remote control aimed at the safe, like a Luger deforming a raincoat. A loud beep and the safe's door opened in two, revealing files, cases of floppy disks, pink and black strapped folders, then a leather case containing a sapphire necklace belonging to Eve Blondel, her two solitaires, her diamond-pearl pinky rings and her Breitschwanz choker. Blondel undid the strap of a pink folder and spread out several blueprints on his desk, charts, comparative tables. Have a look.

Even if he's more familiar with propulsion systems than with propelled vehicles, Meyer knows as well as anyone how to read this kind of thing. He saw immediately that the new Sismo was, in fact, a huge leap forward: its increased resolution would allow it to take bearing of an object twenty times smaller than before, its stereoscopic acuity being improved in proportion. Laser measurement collection, perfect processing of the image on the ground. There it is, said Blondel, the solution.

Eventually, on Earth, a group of self-operating stations would be able to carry out continuous magnetic and gravitational measurements, keeping an eye out for every known precursor to an earthquake. Gathered by Sismo, collector of data, these measurements would complement the information already gathered on the deformations, faults, and folds in the earth's crust. In geostationary orbit above the Mediterranean, the Sismo satellite would meticulously watch over the basin's crust, taking note of the slightest movements in Africa and Eurasia. The real time tracking of fractures and descriptions of the direction and speed of the faults would immediately signal any risk of a large earthquake. There it was, the answer.

— We'll never be able to stop it from shaking, said Blondel, but at least we can order an evacuation before it does. Anyways, I've been waiting for this, it had to move one day or another. It was just what we needed for them to make up their minds. But everything's ready. Sismo is completely ready. I've only got one small detail to work out before sending it up.

— Send it up how? asked Meyer.

— With a small cargo load, as we usually do. Two other satellites, thirty-something experiments on board. They'll even agree, in passing, to let us stop and repair Cosmo.

— Oh yeah, said Meyer, Cosmo.

— Six years it's been in orbit, Blondel reminded him, normal that it has a few problems. We could get it working all right again but we'll have to fix up a couple of things on it. The spectrometer, more than anything else, seems completely out of whack.

— There's no way this is going work, objected Meyer. Three satellites and thirty robots, that's ten times too much for a standard launcher. Even with tiny robots it wouldn't work.

— Who said anything about a launcher? asked Blondel, or about robots? It's all going up on a manned flight. The Americans are lending us an orbiter, we've fixed it up as cheaply as possible. Just a small problem, as I told you, regarding the crew. I'm one man short. I need five and I have four.

He gave Meyer an incredulous look, embarrassed but delighted, as if he'd just become aware of his presence, his utility, as if he'd just understood his potential role, like a fairground exhibitioner secretly rejoicing at the birth of his Siamese triplets.

— You wouldn't be interested in coming? he ventured. A quick week in orbit, don't you feel like giving it a shot? Of course, as you well know, our budget's a bit tight. It wouldn't be very well paid.

17

— You must be joking, Meyer said loudly, I don't have enough training for something like that. And I'm too old for it anyways.

— But you applied to do it, Blondel exclaimed excitedly as he pushed his dog out of his lap to open his suitcase and take out a document. I have the paper, here, you signed it, you passed all the tests. You'd even begun the training.

— That was a long time ago, Meyer said softly, fifteen years ago. Space, we were all up for it. What am I saying, fifteen years. Twenty years is more like it.

— What are you saying? cried Blondel. You'll see, the training's not such a big deal. A quick month and it's over.

Meyer shook his head while loosening his belt a notch, repeated that he was too old and glanced downward, out the window, onto a green and yellow checkerboard cereal field. Besides the pilot up front in a slightly dirty white suit, they were alone above Beauce, surrounded by the hum of propellers and the din of the royal blue Piper Cheyenne's engine. Dakota the dog lay between them, sprawled out in the aisle. This wasn't the first time Meyer had dealt with the animal: bloodshot eyes, long quivering snout, sharp and abnormally irregular incisors, and a wormlike ringed tail decidedly more reminiscent of the rodent order than the carnivore. Blondel brushed aside the age argument, arguing that the guys, normally, in the shuttles, look at the Americans, they're never the young, young ones, haven't you noticed?

And Meyer would truly be the ideal subject. A graduate of the École Polytechnique, and so already militarily trained, he'd also know how to oversee experiments in a variety of scientific fields, chemical or biological, mechanical, medical; and that's without mentioning that the orbiter's propulsion system, one hundred percent carbon silicate, matched his specialty in ceramic engines.

— This orbiter, Meyer wanted to make clear, you're at least sure that it functions all right?

— Perfectly, said Blondel, it was already in very good working condition, and we've refurbished it completely, of course.

Dakota vomited silently at his feet and then began rolling through his own mess, just as repugnant and slow as always— though, endowed with unforeseen impulses, he suddenly jumped onto the knees of a nauseated Meyer. Brusquely pushed away, the giant rat buried back into its vomit. They love knees, these little beasts, Blondel commented joyously.

Meyer turned back toward the window and wiped himself off while the other continued: the most delicate part of this whole affair had been, of course, the fundraising. The ministry gives its support, but as it always is with financial matters it's the bare minimum. They'd had to call a lot of people, sign contract addendums, reach an agreement on the secondary rights: businesses, several television stations, even a little brand advertising. Brand advertising, there's no getting away from that anymore.

Below, the landscape had started to become just a little more mountainous, slightly undulating massifs, soft foothills filled with dark forests. The Piper Cheyenne, gliding along at a low altitude, sometimes skimmed past the summits of rounded hills, so close that you could leap on top of them with neither parachute nor bodily harm. Then, somewhere above Armagnac, when a fertile-looking valley dotted with vibrant colors and surrounding a limestone plateau came into view, they began their descent.

Rudimentary were the airfield's facilities: a single cemented runway, a large striped windsock, a corrugated iron shed on the roof of which, in enormous letters, someone had painted the name of the tiny aerodrome. Another Piper, a sky blue Apache, sitting at the end of the runway; a large dark Peugeot parked near the shed; no onlookers. Out of the airplane, Meyer followed Blondel and Dakota, skirting the shed then climbing into a car, which turned back toward the already airborne Cheyenne.

Heading toward the limestone plateau, they would first pass through the valley, fertile and well irrigated, punctuated by large fancy farms, cozy horticultural establishments. On a large-scale and at full capacity, flower cultivation seemed to be the area's principal source of income. On both sides of the road grew fields of shrub roses, multiflora roses, centifolia roses, gallica roses and Tea roses, the James Masons with the Paul Nérons, the Old Glories, the Virgo Liberationems.

Twenty-five tortuous minutes on a sloping back road, all twists and turns, made Dakota burp noisily and drool over the backseat. Then to the left onto a large, smooth road made of precast concrete, straight, sinking into a chalky canyon. A well-maintained road, reinforced below ground for high tonnage transportation and as empty as a private driveway, a pale canyon to either side on which were scattered groups of thorn bushes, poorly shaved conifers, and then barbed wire in aesthetic complicity. They stopped. A tall high-voltage barbwire wall, solid wire mesh arched every five meters by poles curved at their tops. A large red and white electric gate, inspired by customs, flanked by blockhouse-style sentry boxes and decorated with a large dissuasive pictogram.

Signaled by Blondel with a remote control, the gate gently moved aside along its railing then they were off again on the sparse dry limestone, still populated with hostile thorn bushes, with unpleasant brambles and thistles that nastily watch you go by. Two birds of prey also watched over the area from the sky; sometimes from the shoulder a sacrificial rabbit spurted out, stealthily as if powered by compressed air, into the wheels of the car.

The canyon opened up after a wide turn, they emerged onto a plateau from where they could at last see the training center. Simultaneous appearance of an old motel and an old military camp, past its prime, deconsecrated, recycled into the paramilitary. Three lines of low buildings, a series of bungalows with faded green and beige shutters, flaking, aluminum door handles dotted with oxide, reliefs of very distant and half-hearted attempts at cultivation in front of certain doors—translucent zinnias, degenerate cosmos. Beyond rose up a hangar, ogival with a wavy surface, then another large white building, tiled, cubic and more recent, with no visible doors or windows. That's where the principal machines are, Blondel pointed out. I see Truphème.

In the hour that followed, Meyer went through offices, meeting rooms, bedrooms, all slightly damp though very well lit. He met the administrative people—the lieutenant-colonel Truphème with his secretary Lydie, quartermaster Boeuf, Marie-Madeleine the cook and her two assistants, and the three handymen—and then was assigned to the first bungalow in camp 2. Blondel gave him some time to unpack his things, his very few things, much less than for Marseille, before taking him to the white building. There Blondel would present Meyer to the center's technicians and behaviorists. It was also there that Meyer would come across his future flight commander, onsite since the day before yesterday: commander Bégonhès, a sturdy, smiling native of Pau, with a calm, competent, reassuring attitude. Glasses, mustache, slightly balding. Strong Pau accent. Family man and a light baritone. A little empty in the eyes nevertheless, his gate just a tiny bit unsteady. Doesn't his stare seem just a tiny bit vacant, Meyer inquired in a low voice after Bégonhès had finally managed to find the exit. That's the least of it, whispered Blondel, he just came out of the centrifuge. You'll see.

He showed Meyer the machines, the orbotron, the tilt table,

the catapults, and the hypobaric chamber. Then they visited, in the basement, the swimming pool where they would train for weightlessness by reproducing every situation encountered in flight. Being in water is a little bit like being in space, Blondel informed him, it's a good exercise, you float the same way. We can reproduce everything in the pool except for the fear of dying.

— Departure in exactly one month, he announced three hours later, what are you having? I think quenelles are the daily special but you can also have steak, of course. The daily for me, he ordered like a regular.

The mess was situated in the north wing of the last barracks, oilcloth over the tables and the flight club's bar at the back, trophies and pennants among the bottles, framed photos behind the counter. Meyer and Bégonhès having opted for the steak, Blondel then explained the reasoning behind this date: the alignment of the planets would be opening in exactly one month from now, a twenty-hour window that they ought to take advantage of. Then some information on the flight plan, the crew: besides Bégonhès at the controls with the assistance of another pilot, present in the craft would be two scientists—including Meyer—as well as a civilian who would arrive at the camp tomorrow.

— A civilian, repeated Bégonhès.

— A politician, said Blondel, some parliament member. We're more or less obliged to for the funding. It makes up almost a third of our supplementary budget. It's the toy present in the washing machine of dough, if you get my drift.

As for the pilot, DeMilo, nothing not to like about him, said Blondel. Efficient, he knows his job well. Always in a good mood, charming, must have a million stories about women. He and the other scientist, a biologist named Blanche, were already onsite at the other end of the ocean, at the launch site, training in a camp similar to this one. They've got good weather, smiled Bégonhès. They've got mosquitoes, said Blondel, coffee? We won't start the training right away but if you want, just to see, we can try out a machine this afternoon. If there's nothing else to do, said Meyer.

Stiff the next morning, Meyer found himself a copy of the flight program. Back in bed until past ten o'clock, he read it over several times. Besides the deployment of the Argo and Sismo satellites and the sending off of a spy satellite, his mission responsibilities would include the monitoring, alongside Blanche the biologist, of the usual procedures—dynamics of droplets and perspiration of rice, air-liquid interface and growth of crystals, study on kinetosis. No idea what that is, kinetosis. As always they'd have some animals on board, three guinea fowl from Japan, thirty jellyfish and two rats; some seeds, a crystallizer. The ghost head, a recent addition. They'd have to watch over all this without forgetting to take a routine look outside, to make sure that we're still alone in the universe. Nothing too difficult, no witchcraft required.

After the daily special, Meyer tried out some of the other machines, passing from one to another without getting too exhausted. At the mess hall with Bégonhès, come evening, they talked propulsion throughout the aperitif then, joined by Blondel, they sat down to eat again: red cabbage, kidneys. They'd just received, announced Blondel, a fax from the ministry confirming the civilian's arrival the following day. From then on out, the real training would begin. Then, at the risk of darkening the mood, Blondel thought it good to bring up what life would be like in the orbiter: you will live, he told them, in fear.

18

I know Lucie quite well, the two of us have a long history together. Her bouts of depression, her mood swings, her qualms and doubts and fits of vapors, I know. This doesn't stop me from wanting her. Settled into my canvas armchair on the terrace of the bar des Palmistes, I devote all my attention to her, it's midnight. Jet lag or sulkiness, Lucie doesn't seem to be in the best of shape. But I'm not too concerned about her, and above all I won't give up. I'm patient. I've got all the time in the world.

Around us, certain tables are occupied by technicians from the Center, by engineers on assignment. Some of these ground dwellers recognized me, few of whom gave any sign of acknowledgement, though some of them kept their eyes on Lucie for a moment. This is the first time she's been to Cayenne. No sentimental journey through the tropics, alas, we're here for work. Though the program for the coming days isn't too heavy: tomorrow, for example, nothing. I'll make use of the time to stop by the museum and see the paintings Max told me about, local pieces of interest, by Lagrange and Huguet, former penal camp convicts.

Once again I wouldn't have the time, unfortunately, to take a pirogue tour through the hinterland. But the next day, the museum taken care of, I offered to take Lucie to have a chicken *au couac*, on the road to Tonnegrade, in a Land Rover borrowed from the Center. Dressed in a short-sleeved dress shirt with yellow stripes from Hilditch & Key, I stopped by to pick her up at the end of the morning. While eating, I asked out of politeness—never could stand the guy—how Charles-Henri was, and Lucie responded very quickly that he was doing fine; then, starting again more casually, she told me that they'd broken up. I'd met him two or three times, Charles-Henri, I'd never thought much of the relationship, but still I showed surprise. Although delighted inside, I forced myself to seem sorry. In the afternoon, to distract Lucie, to try and console her, I'd take her to visit what was left of the penal colony on the islands.

In the helicopter that serves Île Royale, Lucie dozed off for several minutes on my shoulder. I made no reaction. As I've said, I've known her a long time; despite my unquestionable interest in her, I've gotten used to being, before anything else, nothing more than a colleague, then a friend, then a kind of confidant, without ever managing to reach the next level. This isn't due to a lack of desire. Nor even, sometimes, of having tried. Attempts always gently declined, as if it was nothing at all, as if Lucie hadn't even noticed. Maybe at bottom, despite our almost fraternal relationship—the worst thing that, taking my desires into account, could have happened to me— maybe she's suspicious of my reputation as a ladies' man, a man who gets his pleasure from that of women. Now, I wouldn't give up. But, this time, I didn't react.

Afterward we walked beneath the coconut palms on the paved trails that go around the island, followed by howler monkeys up above and furtive agoutis at our feet. We talked about various things, mostly professional, but my thoughts were more on the emotional. I already knew, I'd heard it, that things weren't going so well between her and Charles-Henri. Through one of the agency's little secretaries I'd even heard talk of a certain Paul, a recent appearance in Lucie's schedule—but she wouldn't even reveal that much to me this time. I refrained from coming back to her love life, I asked no further questions, even though I was still preparing, once again, to try my luck.

We went along deciphering the graffiti written on the ruins and graves, walking past the remains of the pigsty, the madhouse, the children's cemetery—brick buildings engraved with the initials of the French welfare services, Lucie pointed out. No, I corrected as I took her hand, of the penitentiary administration. But noticing a group of orchid bushes nearby, she gently withdrew her hand under the pretext of bouquet. As if it was nothing. Always the same story.

But I wasn't going to play along with her little game. Putting on my charming smile, I frankly declared, Lucie, you know my number if you change your mind. She smiled as if I hadn't said a word.

19

THEY'D BEEN WOKEN UP early so they could retake the tests. They'd start everything again from zero. Even Bégonhès, despite his experience, had to once again undergo the battery of perceptive, cognitive, and projective tests, although the description of his personality—quick-tempered but methodical—had long been tucked away in his file. Meyer, to begin with, found himself seated for an hour inside a cubicle before a white wooden table, a lead pencil in his right hand as he scratched his head with the left. Then he had to share his thoughts on several inkblots presented by a bony woman with a small mouth, a long pinched nose, a pantsuit made of some rough fabric and four layers of necklaces—a layer of steel for the stopwatch, a layer of plastic for the glasses, and two gold layers for herself. Marking down on a steno pad Meyer's slightest hesitation, she expressed herself with mechanical orders, not looking him in the eyes, from behind the insulation panels of her glasses, any more than one looks a car in its headlights, a robot in the diodes. He tried two or three times to lighten the atmosphere, an attempt at connivance, some harmless flirtation, but all in vain. A little bit like Mercedes, maybe, but not nearly as attractive.

While the behaviorists, decoding the steno pad, peered into Meyer's mind, two other technicians dipped his body into a resin bath to make him a custom bunk, fitted as closely as possible to the resulting mold. They already had Bégonhès's measurements; before exempting him from the resin, they made sure they hadn't changed.

— The test lady's a dragon, Meyer denounced during lunch. A dragon.

— Danièle's a decent girl, Blondel countered, you just have to get to know her a little. She's from Pau.

— Oh really? said Bégonhès.

— Yes, said Blondel, well, at least, I think her mother's family is from Pau.

— An iceberg, Meyer insisted, contact impossible, I tried everything. Not even this much of a smile. (He set down his knife and clicked his thumbnail against an upper incisor.) Not even that.

— The others are like that as well, said Bégonhès, you'll see. Not the best conversationalists. And then there's a shortage of girls, did you notice?

— Danièle's father's side, on the other hand, they're from the Vosges, I believe, Blondel resolutely carried on. And you, Louis, where were you born?

— Plymouth, Meyer responded. But we didn't stay.

— And yourself, Molino?

Paris, said the civilian.

In his double-breasted suit, the civilian hadn't proven to be very chatty. After hello, a pleasure, steak salad, Paris was the sixth word they'd heard come out of him. A smooth and rested face, icy, hair frozen toward the back, strong bracing eau de toilette, he seemed ready for a televised debate. Molino had of course greeted everyone upon arrival, but with a somewhat distant politeness, slightly amused, vaguely skeptical as if there'd been some kind of mistake. Or as if he was taking a walkabout, shaking hands and looking around himself in every direction, trying to spot the camera; even while eating the politician seemed to be waiting for his TV appearance, killing time by having lunch with the stagehands.

The meal finished, he took out a small comb from his pocket before following the others into the hangar, a vast arching Barnum & Bailey-sized space. Almost as many spotlights as Barnum & Bailey, but instead of trapezes hung a black mass in the shape of a boxcar, held in the air by hydraulic jacks and telescopic arms. Torrents of splicing ran out from it, bundles of twisted cables linking it to the technicians' control panels.

— There's the simulator, said Blondel, that's it. We won't be using it right away, I just want to show you the cab.

A slatted freight elevator allowed access to the cab, which was sealed by a metal door with a wheel in the middle, like a safe inside a submarine. Then the simulator's interior, twinkling with a thousand lights, faithfully replicating a space plane's cockpit: control consoles, monitors and keyboards, gauges, levers, radar altimeter and rudder bar. Three covered portholes, two bunks in the back. A strong odor of industrial cleaning products poorly masking vague odors of gyms and must lingering in the air. Blondel introduced the machine: fifty mathematical models managing the system allowed it to simulate anything one could ask for, the good and the bad, the bad more often than the good. The cab's usages were thus multiple: flight simulator, of course, but also pressurized module, thermal chamber, and confinement area. Everyone has a different preference. It's a matter of opinion.

Though let me reassure you, he said, we've decided to lighten the schedule. The amount of sensory deprivation, above all, has been considerably shortened. But we can't go completely without it, unfortunately it's still necessary. Why unfortunately? Molino broke in. Which brings the word count to eight.

At dinner, while Blondel went over some things regarding the orbiter, the politician made manifest efforts to listen, to patiently follow along. Professional technique, old habit beaten in by the campaign trail, as if it was necessary to undergo this to be assured of getting through the first round of elections. But without asking any questions, without appearing concerned, laughing far too shrilly at the wrong moments, sometimes at a not especially funny detail. He seemed far away from these stories of aviation, absent, elsewhere, maybe back amongst his constituency. He took his leave as soon as dinner was finished, without waiting for coffee, please excuse me, cardboard smile, acting as if he had something much more important to attend to elsewhere. Oh come on, thought Meyer.

— He doesn't seem to understand what he's gotten himself into, he observed after Molino's departure, it's like he doesn't give a shit. But he's still going up. He should try to show some interest.

— It's because he's already afraid, Blondel diagnosed, he's dying of fear. That's why.

— Not sure he'll manage the trip so well, worried Bégonhès. Why's he coming, anyways? They couldn't find someone else?

— We can't get rid of him, said Blondel. He's here as a matter of form, but we're obligated. We were a little worried at first, we didn't know what to do with him. Because we had to find something to keep him busy. Vuarcheix's the one who came up with the idea. It's expressly for him that we inserted that last protocol into the experiment list, you know, the little program on kinetosis.

— Excuse me, said Meyer, on what?

— Kinetosis, Blondel repeated. Motion sickness. I'm afraid he'll be of greatest use by being sick, Molino. You'll be able to, well, you'll have to observe him.

20

HELMETED DEEP-SEA DIVER, Meyer is strapped into his ergo-nomic armchair, indicators slid into every orifice, covered with electrodes taped directly to his skin and fitted with sensors trans-mitting data to the behaviorists: heart rate, blood pressure and oxygenation, pulmonary ventilation and all the other gradients. It's not comfortable but it's still going all right, though Meyer's having difficulty with the immobilizing straps. He'd like them to be taken off. He'd feel better without them.

It's still going more or less all right until a symphony of rum-bling gets triggered, scathing sirens and shrill grating, cracking rather reminiscent of the earthquake's soundtrack but ten times louder. All this racket rises toward a crescendo in the confined space of the cab: soon it's not only entering through your ears, it's passing directly through the cranium then spreading through your bones, preferring the unobstructed avenues of the skeleton to the narrow corridors of the nervous system. An overcome Meyer, saturated by noise, quickly loses any sense of his interior and exterior selves, no longer controls his own interface and feels himself get knocked over by a new wave, earth and sky forgotten, cardinal points scattered. Only his reasoning remains somewhat intact, high up in its manhandled case; from the top floor of his body it continues to emit a small ray, weakened but determined, like the optic of a lighthouse spinning in the eye of a cyclone. This, this is the first day.

The second day, same thing.

The third, the uproar at its strongest, it's the cab itself that begins to flail. Without warning it jumps in every direction, sharply, an erratic and frenetic succession of brutal propulsions, increasingly violent jerks that would send the subject to be crushed, if he wasn't secured, against each and every one of the cabin's walls. The noises and the bumping magnify one another, Meyer now thanks God for the straps, prays to heaven that they don't snap, can't think of anything else, almost forgets his desire to vomit.

But more devious still are the behaviorists: on the evening of the fifth day, while speeding the cabin's movements up a notch, with a wide smile they cut the sound. From one moment to the next, not the slightest noise. The vibrations and jolts rage about in a cryptic silence. Invaded by overwhelmingly simple ideas, horrifying, which leave room for little else, Meyer hears nothing more than his rapid breathing, echoed in the suffocating heat of his helmet.

If the returning silence seemed, at first, like a small relief, Meyer will soon understand that in fact it's worse. And that it's even worse still when the cab's movement also cut off. Nothing. And so begin the lengthy stays in confinement, in an absolute deprivation of everything that is, by far, the most trying part of training: it won't be long before Meyer misses the good old days of acrobatics, the hell of stridencies and the fury of impacts, a pleasant Luna Park compared to confinement. No more sound, no movement, an asymptote of death; a strapped-in Meyer has nothing to do but wait, without even the option of counting down the time on the onboard clocks, disconnected by the behaviorists before the session. Still has nothing to listen to, at first, besides his obnoxious, irregular breathing, but his mind soon begins to make a little too much noise as well. Then it's the silence itself, excessively pure, that fathers its own opposite, its deafening negative. Just once, Meyer says something aloud in an attempt to reassure himself, tries to articulate several words, but his voice sounds like something foreign, a ghost machine producing abstract harmonies; he immediately shuts up.

And then of course one must also endure the special sessions in the cab, like when the atmosphere is drastically reduced for example, Everest-like conditions, when you're forced to go searching for crumbs of breath at the bottom of your pockets, in the accelerando of polar and tropical climates. It's hard, but for Meyer it's not a big deal. Nothing compares with solitary confinement in terms of sheer terror.

As soon as they notice that he doesn't like confinement, they begin to double the duration of his sessions. Result: frozen centuries, buried in silence, until an unease begins to form throughout Meyer's mind, an anxiety escorted by waves of nausea, until he begins whimpering while abundantly sweating, then vomiting while screaming, then eventually vomiting while sobbing. To see him break down like this, the behaviorists might be concerned. Not at all. To the contrary they think he's doing just great. Delighted, they multiply the sessions by three, by five, by ten, forcing their subject to renounce this regrettable tendency, this filthy impulse to sully everything while sniveling. And so the subject ends up hardening, learns to remain pure matter, resigned, fatalistic enough to accept the damage, sometimes in a vaguely theistic meditation—recorded no doubt by some special sensor, because immediately the cab flails frantically, sirens wailing, just in time to cut clean his spiritualistic wandering.

At the mess hall, before dinner, Meyer takes a moment to consider the glass in his hand, the sound of the ice cubes; then, as he leans against the bar, the gin and tonic tastes like iron. Pastis for me, Bégonhès orders as he comes up beside him. Cheers. Are you okay? Not too hard? I'll be fine, responds Meyer as he takes an unfriendly sideways glance at the behaviorists, but it seems they no longer know how to piss me off.

At the back of the mess, the behaviorists discreetly put down kirs and bitters, keeping to themselves. They've taken off their lab coats, they're wearing jackets with synthetic polo shirts, they're all in decent shape. They speak quietly, forcing tight smiles, some sport chinstrap beards, one of them has fur-lined, zip-up snow-boots. They keep to themselves. It's a dirty job, but somebody's got to do it. Well aware of their poor reputation among their subjects because of what they force them to undergo, sometimes frightened by the possibility of retaliation, the behaviorists prefer to tread carefully. Interact as little as possible with the flying men outside of the training sessions. Casually ignore, should it settle on them, Meyer's resentful stare.

And Bégonhès himself isn't in top form either, he also endures his fair share of suffering from the behaviorists. Because he spends four or five hours every day in the simulator, required to manipulate his controls like a virtuoso, harassed by short commands coming in rapid succession, sometimes blindfolded, arpeggiating the slides and switches without being able to consult the score.

Not such bad chaps, he says all the same, raising his pastis in their direction. They're just doing their job. One of them has a house near Pau. Have they put you through the centrifuge? The behaviorists smile hopelessly and politely lift their glasses in return. They know that no one ever loves their executioner, even if there's a good citizen, an excellent neighbor, or a loving father beneath the hood. Not yet, says Meyer, I think it'll be the day after tomorrow.

But let's not talk about the centrifuge, a little pod at the end of a spinning arm upon which boards an anxious subject. Then the pod begins turning swiftly at the end of the arm, tossed constantly about by a combination of pitching and rolling: in twenty seconds the subject ages ten years. And let's not talk about the orbotron, a polymuscular machine in which one feels, on certain days, as comfortably settled as one would inside the drum of a washing machine, other times no less at ease than in the trunk of a bumper car. And let's not talk about the rotating seat either, about the multi-axis trainer or the swimming pool, where you're plunged in a diving suit, mechanical claws at the end of your paws, a giant mutant beetle shoved around by black frogmen. Though this might be the most relaxing part, the pool.

All the days unfold identically. Centrifuge upon waking, simulator in the afternoon, during the free moments a little physical education or orbotron. The civilian immediately has difficulties with the simulator, immediately regurgitates his daily special, they don't dare put him in the centrifuge. It's a bad sign, says Bégonhès, that he's already as sick as a dog. They make him spend just a little bit of time in the pool but he still struggles with it. And every evening, they dine at the mess hall with Blondel. Blondel continues assuring them that they'll live in fear, but that fear isn't so terrible. That it's normal and even desirable, that it keeps you awake, that it won't ever stop you from pressing a button. Fear in itself is nothing, he says, it's the fear of being afraid that must be avoided. It's this fear squared, he clarifies, that can destroy you.

21

AND IT SEEMS THAT WE'RE OFF. Stretched out beneath his teflon-kevlar-dacron triple shell, Meyer listens to the nasally countdown. In his peripheral vision, he sees Bégonhès also lying on his bunk, the control panel sparkles more than ever in the opposite corner. As the countdown reaches single-digit numbers and the light in the cockpit dims accordingly, the blast from the nozzles swells in inverse proportion, the control console becomes rapidly excited, synthetic images gallop across the screens. A circle of sunlight passing through the porthole comes to rest innocently on Bégonhès's helmet, Meyer is amazed to be breathing so calmly. Zero, nasals the countdown. Ignition.

Then the exhaust nozzles howl like an organ, almost immediately a long explosion seems to smash against the orbiter's base. The machine wobbles very lightly, just barely tips over to one side before recovering and then rising, heavily, toward the sky. Meyer is flattened with increasing pressure against his bunk, and with increasing speed: the rather large dog that has just jumped onto his chest grows right before his very eyes, in six seconds swells to the size of a young elephant. Despite this Meyer's still breathing okay, still amazed, amazed to hear and understand without too much difficulty the succession of numbers and letters that Bégonhès is exchanging with the technicians at base. It keeps getting heavier, Meyer feels that they're rapidly approaching the threshold of tolerance, then that they've crossed it; but, once past the threshold, it continues to get heavier and heavier. Their powder consumed, the boosters used for take-off detach from the external tank, and the two little jolts from their release transform the baby elephant into a mammoth. Enormous vibrations spread through the cabin. For several seconds, Meyer is happy to lose consciousness. Below him, in midair, the thrusters sway gently at the end of their parachute. On the dark shield of the Caribbean Sea, the white point in the exact center is none other than the tugboat responsible for their recuperation.

The circle of sunlight runs shakily toward the cabin's ceiling then disappears, now only a deep azure disc can be seen through the porthole. The increasingly violent vibrations make Meyer come to, he has to strain the muscles of his eyelids, under the acceleration, to force them apart. Eye-sockets wide open, he feels his features stretch out, go hollow, his smashed cheeks sliding toward his ears, which have for some time now taken refuge behind his neck. The vibrating and shaking continue to grow, it's as if everything's about to explode. Meyer feels arise in his body, in the shape of a crab, the fear heralded every evening by Blondel; he tries to distract himself by focusing to the highest degree possible on the azure disc, which is now darkening to navy blue, then very quickly to Prussian blue then to dark violet then swiftly to black. Too much speed: Meyer suffocates while the crab and the mammoth come together on his stomach, hit it off and make plans for the future. Since they decide, as a start, to have a little fun at Meyer's expense, he prefers to pass out once again.

The menagerie goes wild seven minutes later, when it's the external tank's turn to be cast off; crab and mammoth jump with joy to welcome its disintegration in the ether, falling like fine rain over the ocean. Meyer can no longer summon the strength to open his eyes; beneath his closed eyelids the pressure gives birth to myriad brightly colored phosphenes, to fragmented stars, to stroboscopic crosses and pyrotechnic crescents on a background of stairs and checkerboards. Abandoning himself to the show, he belatedly realizes that the pressure seems to be diminishing, to be loosening its grip. Soon it's not even noticeable, it's gone into hiding; in theory, this is the sign that they've arrived. Because, now beyond the Earth's pull, they've entered orbit, they're floating freely through the silence of space and everything's all right. The elephant's evaporated. The crab keeps more or less quiet. Meyer, however, continues to play dead, even though he's conscious, even though he continues to follow the coded conversation between Bégonhès and base that soon breaks off; then he hears Blondel's voice in his crumpled ear:

— Are you okay?

I'll be fine, Meyer sputters as he opens an eye.

Blondel is leaning over the bunk, looking serious and concerned in his lab coat, squeezing the handle of a small LCD device connected to the sensors. His eyes shift from Meyer's face, distraught behind the window of the spacesuit, to the device's screen and its waltzing parameters. What happened, a little blackout?

— Nothing at all, Meyer says as he tries to move an arm, I'll be perfectly fine. Can I take this off?

Blondel helps him sit up on the edge of the bunk. Two underling behaviorists, as if nothing has happened, come and go through the cockpit's open door. One rewinds the short blue film projected in the porthole, the other helps Bégonhès undo his helmet.

— You're holding up better and better, Blondel points out while undoing Meyer's, your readings are even better than on Friday. We'll do two or three more quick simulations like this one, then you should be able to handle the departure without any problems.

The last fastening undone, Meyer lifts his helmet with as much difficulty as someone ripping their own head off, but an awkward movement makes him drop the object, which collides against his shoulder before rolling toward one of the underling's feet. The man picks up the helmet and looks it over with disapproval.

— Anyways it's just about finished now, continues Blondel, you won't spend any more time in the machines. Just a bit of parachuting as a matter of form. You've already jumped, I believe.

— Ten times when I was younger, Meyer rounds off.

— Perfect, says Blondel. Once is enough, it's like riding a bike. Wait till you see Bégonhès, jumping's like breathing for him.

Parachuting, no doubt, will be the most enjoyable part of training. First they set off by jeep to the airfield then get aboard a Noratlas, which immediately takes off. The aircraft rises to the required height then turns back to fly over a circular target, three hundred meters from the runway, an immense tricolor roundel of brightly colored crushed chalk sitting on the grass.

Not very warm in the Noratlas's hold, and the jump instructor isn't very warm either. Other than pushing people off into the void when the plane passes over the target, his utility isn't very clear. Meyer jumps first, Bégonhès two seconds later, the plane's belly recedes into the distance. The two men fall at the same speed, they move toward one another at first then come apart and go gliding on their separate ways, arms wide open in midair, before opening their canopies, each one in his own little patch of sky.

They pull on the ripcord at the same moment, slamming their brakes in the ether as a bubble of silk blooms above them. Peace rediscovered, silence just barely grazed by the wind. The canopy flaps lightly above them, like a dinghy's sail. They let themselves descend, passing feathered creatures, two buzzards, a bearded vulture swooping down toward a carcass, at one point a whole group of ducks in a V; Meyer almost gets taken in by the V's scissors. Hitched up by large straps, he at first grips the ropes like handles on a bus; then, more relaxed, he crosses his arms over the little frontal reserve container and considers the world at his feet. He sees the limestone plateau tightly encircling the buildings of the training camp, then all around him the prosperous plain, the deep-rooted farms soaking up the fertile humus, the little trucks parked near the fields, the little tractors laboring through the hectares of flowers.

From so high up, the colors of the rose gardens don't stand out so well, but the closer you get the more their tones come into focus, from yellow patches of Baby Masquerade to pink apricot Cupids, to crimson July Orphans and immaculate Botzaris. The Vick's Caprices become more and more distinct from the Rembrandts, one mixes up James Mason and Madame René Coty less and less. Meyer and Bégonhès soon enter their fragrance, the combination of all their fragrances, a large column of invisible smoke rising above the blaze of roses. As if into a pool of warm water they dive into this mass of jumbled scents, which will soon break down into an enormous number of sparkling and spicy variations, of nuances both subtle and strong. And depending on whether one prefers the myrrh of the Splendens, the clove of the Blush Noisette or the primrose of Félicité-Perpétue, depending on whether one wishes on the contrary to avoid the strong musky fragrance of Madame *Honoré Defresne*, you swing accordingly at the end of your parachute toward the color from which arises the desired aroma, you aim for the small plot of extremely rare green roses, the square of Baroness Henriette of Snoy, the rows of Memory of Pierre Vibert or the quincunx of Max Graf.

Of course, in these conditions, one rarely reaches the chalk target. But because the training is coming to an end, let's celebrate with a final bouquet: Meyer allows himself to go among the flowers whose bushes, muffled crunching, slash the silk of his parachute, an infinite number of stockings running on an infinite number of perfumed legs; Bégonhès isn't much more conscientious. Their chutes in the middle of the fields, moreover, never receive a cold welcome from the horticulturists. To the contrary, affable Portuguese men armed with tweezers run up immediately, painlessly extracting the parachutists' thorns while at the other end of the field, from his office window, the grower calculates the damage. Without taking his eyes off them or setting aside his binoculars, he reaches a practiced hand toward the telephone and dials, from memory, the number of his insurer. And so every landing in the roses is a pleasure for all, every party besides the insurer finds the affair excellent. They hit it off with the Portuguese men, they say the three Portuguese words they know, they joke around with them then fold up their parachutes as best as possible before making their way back. The Portuguese lend a hand, accompany you for part of the way, then, as you pass in front of their little seasonal worker's accommodation, the Portuguese suggest coming inside to have a drink; you can't say no.

Feeling rather cheerful forty-five minutes later, they return by foot toward the nearby aerodrome—it's right across the street. As soon as the target comes into view, they also see Blondel standing at its center, straight as a dart in the little red circle. He appears to be waiting, they're a little worried, they don't say anything but they wonder if he's going to chew them out. Not at all. Blondel seems rather content. He himself has stuck a little Deuil de Paul Fontaine into his buttonhole, into which his nose is currently plunged. It's exquisite, he declares, it smells exactly like the packet of tea we just opened. We're leaving tomorrow.

22

MEYER, GUIANA—AT FIRST SIGHT he doesn't really see the attraction, he pictures little more than a tongue of moist dirt teeming with parasites, soaked with fevers and beer-filled soldiers. To launch our rockets, couldn't we have chosen someplace breezier, a bit cooler, still just as French, Saint-Pierre-et-Miquelon, for example? Question of cash, Blondel replied, you know that as well as I do. No point in looking any further. Closer we are to the equator, the faster we get out of the Earth's pull and the less we have to spend on fuel. In any case, Bégonhès reminded him, the beer-filled soldiers adapt equally well to the cold.

Seated next to Meyer, Bégonhès flipped through lists and flight instructions assigned by Blondel before they'd left. Hiding beneath the seat in front of him, Meyer caught sight of a booklet left behind by a previous passenger, an appendix of ballistic data from the user's manual of a ground-to-ground missile. The girl situation doesn't seem to be getting better, Bégonhès calmly smiled.

On this issue indeed no improvement. No attendants aboard this new plane, an army-issued Lockheed C-130 Hercules, no pink champagne or movie projected in eight languages, no reclining armchair or adjustable reading light, no business class in-flight meal with quadrichromic menu, nothing. Just the loud rumbling noise of the Hercules's engine, eight seats bolted in

pairs beneath a harsh light at the back of the cabin, behind piles
of containers covered in stenciled pictographs, and a slightly
mocking conscript, uniform sleeves rolled up above his elbows,
who gracelessly set down a military ration on Meyer's lap, energizing fruit leather for dessert.

Boredom soon rearing its ugly head, the conscript supplied
them with thirty-two playing cards advertising Granier pastis,
which Meyer rhythmically shuffled. Thank you, but I don't play,
said Blondel after the civilian had also declined with a weak
shake of the head, I don't know anything about cards. You guys
aren't very nice, said Bégonhès, it's always less interesting with
two. What do you think of making the game a little more interesting, Louis? And he seems a bit pale, Molino, don't you think?

Bégonhès would lose three hundred francs before giving
up then dozing off in his seat, exhausted. Meyer followed suit
shortly after, only Blondel went on consulting his folders on the
other side of the aisle: confused by such an enthusiasm for work,
Dakota lay strewn against him panting ceaselessly, his long snout
gaping open like a cooked mussel, raptly watching his master
and letting a skinny dry yellowish tongue flop out. Alone on a
seat behind them, the civilian held a handkerchief to his lips.

Ten interminable hours went by, falling asleep, waking
up, sometimes spent in the grease of a meal, perseverance
through the torpor, expressionless faces, fewer and fewer words
exchanged, without a smile they pass around the bag of salt.
They lifted heavy eyelids during the refueling stop at Fort-de-
France, palm trees through the windows, certainly far too hot,
no time to see much anyways, Meyer wouldn't even leave his
seat. Having gotten off to stretch his legs a bit on the tarmac,
Bégonhès came back into the plane dripping with sweat. Quite
hot indeed, he confirmed. It's not going to be easy. They took
back off.

23

ONE HOUR LATER I WAS WAITING for them at the bottom of the plane's ladder. DeMilo, exclaimed Blondel, how nice of you to come and get us. He presented Meyer and Molino, both of whom I'd heard a bit about, neither the former nor the latter very talkative. After which Bégonhès and I patted each other on the back.

I'm practically the same age as Bégonhès. Like him, I have a mustache, though he cuts his differently. Same training, same experience, more or less the same qualifications. Both field-proven fighter and test pilots. Him squadron commander and me patrol leader, graduated the same year from the Empire Test Pilots' School with three thousand hours of flying each. But I'm quite certain that I look younger.

I smiled, relaxed, pointed out the white minibus, smiling at them with all my enamel beneath the scorching sun. I'm diligent about maintaining this tanned Californian bachelor appearance—so much so that I'm sure people must imagine that my civilian life, far from interstellar space, is one of beaches, girls, bars, maybe even with a red convertible, filled with girls and parked in front of a bar on a beach. Why not.

Once in the minibus, Bégonhès and I went on expressing our delight at being together again. Beneath the electric blue sky we crossed a flat green expanse of land, dampened by swamps, we were soon on the road for Sinnamary. The bus turned toward the

cosmodrome's first entrance as soon as the administrative buildings came into view; further away, scattered near the mangrove,
were the residential buildings for the flight crew.

The bungalow allocated to Meyer was reminiscent of the
one he'd had at the training camp, a tropical version subtitled
with air conditioning, mosquito nets, and extra fans. Meyer lay
down, was unable to sleep, got back up to go look out the windows. Dense vegetation, not very diverse: tall sharp palm leaves,
skeletons of giant fans, formed a thick bushiness up to mid-
thigh. Above, several shrubs barely taller than a hunchbacked
man and then local varieties of holm oaks with thin drooping
branches, cluttered with parasitic lichens and Spanish moss with
grayish eyelashes. The heavy heat was accompanied by a heavy
silence, which was sometimes crumpled by the passage of invisible animals through the depths of the vegetation, small or medium-sized animals, though sometimes producing a rather large
sound. Armadillos and anteaters, tapirs and peccaries, whose
stealthy bursts through the vegetative innards resounded like
peristaltic waves, like elastic knots coming violently unraveled.
Meyer was finally asleep when, two hours later, Blondel came
knocking on his door. The experiments, he said, all the devices
are ready. You can start inspecting them if you're feeling up to it.

Always the same kind of experiments, the same conventional
protocols, formation of nylon, melon respiration, all that stuff.
The highlight of the trip, this time, would be the ghost head,
responsible for testing the penetration of cosmic rays into bone.
The genuine head of a woman, in fact, a real skull bequeathed
to science by its usufructuary, stuffed with devices much more
powerful than itself alone and covered with a synthetic epidermal
film. What are the odds, out of a thousand, that Meyer had met
this woman while she was alive, he briefly wondered, the proba-
bility he'd slept with her? Then he looked over the animals that
would be taken onboard, low-end fauna and much less exotic,
of course, than that of the mangrove. To the initial jellyfish and
guinea fowl from Japan would be added three handfuls of blue

and red maggots along with a spider, plus other small creatures to feed this little herd. One of the rats, manic-depressive, had been causing some problems for the psychophysiologists. If he can't handle it, how can we scrounge up a replacement for him? Blondel jokingly offered Dakota. At his feet, in response to this proposal, the foul creature screeched with pleasure. A nauseated Meyer noticed Bégonhès's mustache shudder. As for myself, my smile flagged. Titov, I thought.

In the evening, we found ourselves on the terrace of Blondel's bungalow, wearing light acrylic suits in florescent magenta, pinned with badges, with passes. The sun was on its way down. The light meal in light pajamas created an atmosphere of convalescence, of being in the dining hall of a scrubland sanatorium. As we would strictly focus, at first, on only the technical, the civilian was excused. Blondel made an initial run over of the experiments, of the repairs to the Cosmo spacecraft and the deployment plans for the three satellites. We would go deeper into all of that tomorrow, after the arrival of Dr. Blanche, the biologist provided to supervise the experiments with Meyer. Well. Do you want to see the aircraft? I do, said Bégonhès.

The jeep went tearing off toward the launch complex, passing the control and weather stations, the buildings for payload preparation. All around us the same green horizontal surface went stretching out, meager, excavated in some places with monstrous holes, bristling in others with the skeletons of construction-in-progress. We drove along swiftly below the moon, the warm air making Blondel's bald head shine and our suits puff out. Soon, in the dark air, past the hydrogen pool and the propellant mixer, the silhouettes of the umbilical tower and service structure materialized in the distance, though there still remained three checkpoints to cross before reaching the launch pad. And there, hanging from the superstructure and covered with three oblong tanks, high above like a cathedral fortified with minarets, the space plane awaited us.

The propulsion systems were being tested: thick chubby

impenetrable clouds bubbled at the bottom of the assemblage while beams of pallid spotlights appeared like huge pieces of chalk in the smoke from the combustion. Rumblings, vibrations, fumaroles. The plane, a white isosceles triangle, sat hooked up to the giant tank, painted pale green and flanked by two bright pink boosters: pointed at their tips, the orbiter and its three engines were packed between nine floors of tubular networking, compact scaffolding made up of metal beams. On the structure's platforms, in the clamor of the engines, swarmed the helmeted workers, dressed in golden yellow suits and deafened by sound isolation earplugs. Blondel handed out earplugs while we looked on, heads tipped back as if at the foot of a skyscraper; the machine roared a moment more then sluggishly fell quiet, giving way to indistinct orders, very high up, in the walkie-talkies, to muddled injunctions that went bouncing between platforms. Bégonhès wanted to go up and look but no, said Blondel, not now, several fixtures were still missing from the mid-deck. Better to visit the completed complex, when everyone would be there, tomorrow morning.

Last drink at the bar des Palmistes before going to lie down, quiet conversation, a decent amount of people on the terrace. A dreamy Bégonhès didn't say much. Since I found the boosters' colors a little reminiscent of a baby's bedroom, I let it be known. I hope Molino's not going to spend the whole time throwing up on us, I complained afterward. Don't worry, said Blondel, we'll fasten him up. Meyer was also off daydreaming in his armchair, sucking up small mouthfuls from the end of his punch, permeable to the surrounding voices, to the laughter from the nearby tables, to the gusts of international pop songs coming and going like scarves swinging in the sticky air, which come and go now everywhere, in the supermarkets, through the mangroves, inside igloos.

Only Blondel had anything to say, never unpleasant to listen to, although this thing about fear, wasn't he starting to get a little repetitive? Then he talked about the vanity of all this, the price of all that. He explained once again how difficult it is to finance this kind of operation, to get funding from firms, from laboratories, not to mention marginal budgeting, for example the little contracts he'd managed to sign with the TV companies. While we're on the subject, DeMilo, he said, did you think about the relay over Hawaii? Everything's ready, I replied. Below the table, in an outburst of total satyriasis, Dakota had thrown himself onto his back, trembling, stomach on display and paws folded, do me please do me, I pushed him away with the tip of my shoe.

Meyer wasn't afraid the next morning, still not afraid while we were on our way toward the launch pad. The civilian sat in the back of the jeep, in-flight suit and matching helmet just like the rest of us. A little too big for him, his helmet tried to fly off several times during the journey, its visor flapping like a wing in the hot air. We stopped, reversed, I jumped gracefully over the door onto the tips of my nylon boots, went to recuperate Molino's headgear from the bug-infested ditches, then we were off again. We finally reached the security gate at the foot of the vessel, we drove toward a small parking lot marked off by plastic ribbon where Poecile the engineer seemed to be waiting, short-sleeved dress shirt and gray protective helmet, worried eyebrows, also gray. Without a glance at the rest of us he immediately addressed Blondel, who was pulling the parking break, cutting the ignition. Dr. Blanche isn't with you?

— My God no, responded Blondel, I thought the doctor would meet us here.

— At any rate, her car's not here, said an irritated Poecile as he looked over the parking lot and then at his watch. This is going to delay things.

We'll wait for her up above, Blondel decided. Let's go.

He pointed out the entry to the service elevator, a deep massive iron box: we piled in. Blondel came in last and clarified that we weren't going to visit the orbiter right away, first we'd make a stop to examine the locking system on the engines. The elevator rose very slowly then braked very slowly, halfway up

the scaffolding. We went out in silence onto the platform surrounding the space plane, already we were very high up, very
far from the ground.

A nervous wind swept through the skybridge, one of those
feisty little winds unhappy about not being able to create as
much damage as it would like, that would love to cause more
serious destruction to things, to the men clinging onto the
earth—one of those nasty little winds that takes its revenge as
soon you get a little higher, trying to throw you off balance with
sharp, sudden blows, perniciously aimed below the belt or at the
eyes. Even Bégonhès and myself, not prone to vertigo, held onto
the guardrail and avoided looking down. The civilian, of course,
had immediately decided to madly embrace one of the platform's
pillars, as desperately as if it were his own mother. Only Blondel,
holding onto nothing, bent over to admire the view. Taking
Meyer by the arm, he gave a tour of the skybridge, pointing out
the components for stowage, then for release of the fuel tank
and the supplementary detonators. The orbiter's fuselage had
clearly seen better days: its surface was spotted with touch-up
paint jobs, with little craters caused by the collisions it'd been
subjected to, most of them originating from encounters, during
its previous missions, with various debris from other spacecrafts.
Blondel bent back over toward the void after the inspection, two
white locks fluttering about his temples:

— Ah, he said, I believe that's the doctor's car pulling up. I
see her. Do you see her?

— Yes, Poecile confirmed after a cautious glance. That's her.

Send down the elevator for her, said Blondel. We'll wait here.

The elevator started back down as slowly as it'd come up. The
civilian hadn't moved from his pillar, still desperately embracing
it, a line of acidic saliva slid from a corner of his mouth toward
the tip of his chin. While Bégonhès and I looked over the new
riveting procedure on the boosters, Meyer lifted his eyes toward
the belly of the plane, covered, like the wings and nose, with a
mosaic of ceramic tiles, shiny and grainy like a lizard's abdomen.

He distractedly lent an ear to the unhurried elevator machinery—click: the cables came to a halt; new click: they rewound in the other direction.

Last click: a red warning light came on above the sliding doors, which began, still just as slowly, to separate from one another. Meyer watched as Blondel cracked a sugary smile, let go of the railing, and then moved toward the elevator, followed by Bégonhès and myself, both of us as delighted as he was to be back with the doctor. A pale Molino, eyes rolled back into his head, seemed to make an attempt to let go of his pillar. Poecile smiled as well, throwing a forgiving glance at his watch and moving to join them, blocking Meyer's view of the elevator, who, in turn, decided to go toward it, at first concealed by Bégonhès's large shoulder blades. Bégonhès then having moved over, Meyer found himself face to face with the young woman. This is unexpected. No one had warned him.

So unexpected that it takes him a moment to recognize her, this young woman opening surprised eyes then looking at him with confusion as Blondel introduces them:

— Lucie, this is Louis Meyer, whom I've talked to you about, I believe. Meyer, this is Dr. Blanche.

— Mercedes, Meyer pronounces slowly.

Excuse me? says Blondel.

24

THERE ARE WOMEN THAT YOU only meet again in elevators. And there are men, like the civilian, who seem to be of great interest to this type of woman, Meyer thinks on the jeep ride back. It's none of my business, but I'd like to know what they could possibly see in him. Especially next to a handsome guy like me, his thoughts specify a little while later, at lunch, as he breaks the heart of a palm.

Back from the launch pad, at the cosmodrome's first-class mess hall, Meyer sits at the corner of a table; to his left Bégonhès rolls a ball of crumbs, increasingly spherical and gray, between his fingers. I've settled down across from them next to a distracted Blondel, his rat terrier sprawled out on his lap: I listen to Poecile, who's left his helmet on to eat, describe the planned deployment of the spy satellite. Having become perfectly black and round, the ball ends up rolling onto the floor and Dakota pounces off after it straight into the doctor's and the civilian's feet, seated next to each other in a blind spot to the left of Bégonhès. Molino, it seems, is quietly chatting up Mercedes, who responds just as quietly and who should no longer, now, be referred to like that. Their conversation is difficult to make out. Stuck between a mute Blondel and a mute Bégonhès, Meyer recites Lucie Blanche Lucie Blanche Lucie Blanche to get himself accustomed to this new identity in the humming of the big fan.

If the young woman, coming out of the elevator, appeared

to have a hard time identifying Meyer, afterward she seemed determined to recognize him less and less. Here she goes, he'd said to himself, here she goes again just like when we were down south. They didn't exchange a single word during the tour of the orbiter. She kept herself at a distance from Meyer, who, for his part, displayed an extreme interest in the smallest details of the capsule's layout—though, his thoughts being preoccupied, he didn't understand a word of Poecile's explanations. But before all that, the elevator having arrived at the top floor, Blondel had broken off into a quick speech at the threshold of the airlock, stopping the group before entering the space plane.

— Your indulgence, he'd appealed for, I'm warning you that not everything is entirely spotless. This is a spacecraft that's already been through a fair share of missions. It's been very kindly lent to us but we haven't been able, unfortunately, to refurbish it entirely. I hope I have your understanding.

The crew furrowed their eyebrows, Blondel had to qualify his statement. Of course they'd redone all the fundamentals, completely updated the insulation, tested the circuits, carefully reviewed the forty-five different engines, the twenty-three antennas and the five onboard computers, no problems in that respect. The safety devices had also been the object, of course, of careful scrutiny, nothing to worry about there either. But, well, there wasn't enough time to do a good, thorough housecleaning. We were in a bit of a hurry, let's not forget, the alignment of the planets favorable for departure wouldn't last forever, the weather window would only be open for some twenty or so hours. Naturally the biggest things have been taken care of, but the windows, for example, well, you'll see that that's not the case at all. Shall we continue. Lucie?

With Meyer far from Lucie and Molino soon to be close behind her, we went into the plane through the flight deck, the first level consisting of the flight and central control room, the principal navigation instruments. Almost the same as the simulator but with a dual control system: two chairs facing two instrument panels, screens and closed-circuit cameras, huge candy box consoles with every flavor of flashing light. I went straight to the control panel on the right, which would be assigned to me. I inspected the device with small confident movements, carefully casual, distractedly pushing back a slider, testing the accessibility of a lever with the tips of my fingers, exchanging a few reluctant words with Bégonhès who'd come and sat down in the chair to my left. The others watched us for a moment, then Blondel proposed visiting the next level.

Still a good distance from Lucie Blanche, the civilian following in her wake, Meyer preferred to wait with us until Bégonhès got up, not without a little pout. Well, I suppose it'll be okay, he grumbled, we'll try to get it off the ground. With the same attitude I shrugged my shoulders, then without another remark we went to join the others on the mid-deck. That's where we'd be living.

— You've got the bunks over there, Blondel indicated, and then here you have the shower. You have two, no, three cabinets here, you can see that they're quite spacious, also easy to access. Then here's the kitchen with all its products.

The whole interior of the cabin was done up with adhesive loops and strips of Velcro, anchoring points allowing you to secure any variety of things, cans and cameras, documents and bodies—points without which, in zero gravity, pressurized ballpoint pens would escape without having written a word, brushes would run away from hair and teeth alike. Blondel also showed us, stored to one side of the mid-deck, the little *Get Away Special* compartments, containing materials for autonomous experiences. And then at last you have here, he said, pardon me, the area dedicated to relaxation and waste treatment.

— The john, Bégonhès translated as he peered in through the door. To see if there was any graffiti.

And, indeed, there was, which we would be sure to read later on. Followed by further evidence in the corners, discreet food stains or finger smears, proving that they had in fact only done a superficial cleaning of the cabin, without erasing the felt-tip dates and signatures above the bunks, without removing the stickers. There was even a photo of the previous pilot's fiancée still stuck next to the angle indicator for atmospheric reentry, beneath a decorative magnet imitating a package of Dentyne. In any case they could've done the windows, the civilian half-heartedly critiqued.

— Not easy, said Blondel, the metal lets off gases in orbit. They condense on the panes, it's not like water vapor. It's a nuisance to clean. But it shouldn't be too much of a problem. Of course, you can always see what you can do yourselves in flight, all the products are here.

Leaving the mid-deck, we went to see the plane's cargo bay. The satellites we'd be deploying hadn't been loaded yet, but the space scooter, which would allow us to leave the orbiter, was already sitting parked at the back, locked to a post like any old Vespa to a sidewalk street sign. Equipped with twenty or so small compressed-gas rocket engines, we'd use the scooter for extravehicular outings, in particular for repairing the Cosmo engine.

Then as we passed through the mid-deck again before leaving the vessel, Blondel gave a little theoretical reminder. The absence of gravity, in flight, would abolish all pressure, all resistance, things would behave however they pleased. The vertebrae, thus, would no longer weigh upon one another, they'd spread out and cause us to come back from space a little bit taller than when we'd left. Duly pointing out the two exercise machines, a stationary bicycle and a treadmill:

— Indispensable. Thirty minutes of each one per day, he prescribed. Without it your muscles will become completely soft, in three days you'll have chicken legs.

In the elevator, behind Lucie Blanche, the civilian went on giggling as we shared our impressions during the descent. And then at the ground floor, as the doors we're opening, a series of flashes suddenly surged forth from the light outside, five or six all at the same time. Everyone took a step back. It's okay, said Blondel, photographers, come on now. Photographers. Strike a pose. We leave in a week. Normal for them to prepare for the event.

Even if the time of global audiences was over, the time of big firsts, of worldwide all-nighters in front of the TV, of official portraits, your smiling face sticking out of your spacesuit on magazine covers, on post stamps, on key rings. Nobody gives a shit, now. No special correspondents dispatched from far away, the photographers at the elevator door only work for very local rags, some of them are nothing more than interns. Whatever, we struck a pose all the same, everyone assuming an astronaut's attitude to the best of his abilities: Bégonhès in Russian-style, a wide casual smile and a loose-knit undershirt beneath the uniform, robust and cheerful, while I tended toward a more American appearance, more supple and relaxed in my T-shirt, no less cheerful or robust but looking better in the uniform. Poecile had left on his helmet and Blondel his glasses, the civilian made an effort to reproduce the poster from his last cantonal campaign. One second, said the doctor, do I have time to put on some blush?

The doctor: Meyer would still manage to catch her for three almost private seconds before leaving the launch pad, when we stepped back a final time, hands as visors and noses raised, squinting eyes aimed toward the top of the structure. He moved backward toward her: I'm delighted to see you again, he declared simply in a single breath. Not very original, but his heart was in it. But all he got in response was a second helping of icy smile, Dr. Blanche's refreshing specialty; one hour later, at the first class mess hall, a particularly upset Meyer would sit as far away as possible, at the other end of the table.

25

WE'D DO SOME MORE TRAINING in the four days that followed, then seventy-two hours before blast off Blondel put everyone on complete rest, in an aseptic environment sheltered from mosquitoes and intern journalists. Only the details remained to be taken care of. In certain workshops, specialized little hands finished sewing on the innumerable pockets intended to hold pencils and pocketknives, lights, calculators, gloves, sunglasses and energy bars, a wide variety of foreign currencies alongside visa-covered passports, provided in case, should we encounter mechanical trouble, we found ourselves forced to land in some unforeseen country. While other sewers embroidered, on these same pockets, the logos of the businesses sponsoring the flight— Uniroyal, Matra, Liquid Air and Bright Life, a large group of maritime insurance companies, a brand of yoghurts with active bifidus. Nothing more for us to do besides a routine visit to the infirmary two days before departure.

Leading into a nickel-plated corridor, the infirmary's white-tiled, air-conditioned waiting room was exaggeratedly clean, furnished with tubular chrome chairs, rot-proof glass and ceramic, nothing left unattended to, everything shining as if it'd just come out of the box. Piled onto a display rack, an armful of wrinkled magazines, ragged periodicals, reminders that the world is biodegradable. A world silently crossed sometimes by an immaculate nurse, a redemption among the incense of disinfectant. Meyer's eyes would then mechanically follow a fold in the scrubs or the tautness of a snap fastener, watching for illusions of underwear, for allusions to their absence.

Among the periodicals a very old *Express*, two *USA Todays*, a *Terre-Air-Mer* and a month-old *Paris-Match*, a special edition entitled *Marseille: A Farewell* containing photos of funeral processions. Meyer leafed through it, thinking that he recognized a storefront on one of the processions' routes, a storefront glimpsed through the thick dust when he'd left the mall with Mercedes. He closed the magazine when I appeared at the end of the corridor, adjusting one of my suit's cuffs. Your turn, Louis, I said, it's nothing more than a formality. Room 6.

Meyer followed the corridor, softly beating his left palm with the *Paris-Match* rolled up in his right. No response was forthcoming when he knocked beneath the golden metal 6, so he knocked again then opened the door, discovering Lucie Blanche writing behind a table. This was also rather unexpected. Once again no one had warned him.

Booby-trapped, poor Meyer.

She'd raised her eyes in his direction, sliding delicate glasses to the end of her nose to watch him come in. Having changed her training suit for something more summer appropriate, she seemed to be making a quick stop at the office in the middle of a vacation—I'm just taking care of a little thing and then I'm back to the beach. She pointed to the seat on the other side of the table, Meyer looked over the armchair as if it was furnished with chromium steel jaws, ready and waiting to clamp down on him; he hesitated. An examination bed behind him and a stand of medical utensils in dull metal hors d'oeuvres dishes sent a chill down his spine.

— This is the last little check-up, it'll be quick. I'm getting your file, won't you take a seat?

She was bending toward a shelf, her glasses in one hand so she could flip though the crew's files; a very ill at ease Meyer preferred not to watch. So how's it going? she said as one says

twenty times a day. Not bad, he replied, not bad. Then the usual
questions about sleep and circulation, digestion, always somewhat uncomfortable to talk about these kinds of things in front
of women. No appetite or memory loss? No, said Meyer. No
faintness or dizziness from time to time? Well yes, thinks Meyer.
Hotel Negro-Welcome. Eyzin-Pinet. Anyways, she should be
able to remember. But he responds with a no. Nothing to report.

— Perfect, she says, let's make sure that's the case. You can
lie down there, please take off your shirt if it's not too much to
ask. Good.

An anxious Meyer's blood flowed at top speed as he gracelessly unbuttoned. It's beating a little fast maybe, she diagnosed,
speaking into the stethoscope above his naked torso, but the
rhythm is good. I'm going to listen to your chest a little, there.
Yes, he said. But try to relax, you're too tense. Sorry, said Meyer,
frightened to death that she'd then request him to undo his belt,
just so that she could go fishing for lymph nodes in his groin.
But no, nothing like that. And here, she pushed softly, any pain?
I don't think so, said Meyer. He put his clothes back on as she
jotted a couple things down into his file before showing him
out the door.

— Looks okay, she said with an impersonal smile, everything'll be okay. See you tomorrow.

Yes, says Meyer, who now finds himself alone again in the
deserted corridor but doesn't move away, who pauses, eyebrows
furrowed as if trying to understand something, to remember
something at the tip of his tongue. Then he takes a deep breath,
turns back toward the door and reopens it: excuse me, he says
in a hesitant voice, one second. I think I forgot my newspaper.

She turns around, she was looking out the widow, it seems
that she doesn't have quite the same face, a gray slightly sad line
streams by slowly in her eyes. Of course, she says softly. But
instead of hastily scooping up the paper and clearing out, Meyer
closes the door carefully. A more worrisome line, greener, passes
by a little more quickly in Lucie Blanche's eyes when Meyer sets

the paper down onto the desk, flips methodically through it then slides it in her direction open to a photo, a full center spread, showing the mall swarming with rescue workers. We get what he's trying to do, we understand his plan. But we also see that he's emotional, the poor guy, incapable of finishing even half of his sentences:

— You don't remember this, he says, do you? Why don't you, why do you act like I'm, as if we don't?

It's a risky maneuver.

26

A RISKY MANEUVER, BECAUSE after all why complain, and first of all reproach her for what. For doing what. Everyone has the right to be cold. That a common ground shakes beneath our feet in no way implies intimacy. But there's also the fact that Meyer is upset. Also, still very irritated it seems: I wouldn't want you not to have, he strives to expand upon, but I'm curious what I.

Let it go, Louis. Meyer falls silent. As the young woman doesn't respond right away, the only sound to be heard is the hum of the air-conditioning, outside the distant scream of a jay. In barely three seconds of silence, Meyer has time to plead to himself that what he's doing is idiotic, that this could end badly, that the most insignificant thing can ruin the mood on a flight through space and that it'd be regrettable to compromise the mission; yeah but also I don't care, he responds to himself with conviction, people don't treat me like this, I'm irritated, I'm upset, but then we don't want her pulling a fast one and taking it as clinical evidence, a symptom or something like that, she could put me on Tranxene, declare me unfit for orbital flight and then I end up looking like a fool; but I don't care, he reiterates with a little less conviction. All this in three seconds. Then Lucie bursts into tears and collapses into his arms. Of course, that's the only thing to do, Meyer says to himself coldly, that's the best way to behave. But what do I do now.

Now, now, he says, come on. Let's have a seat.

A rather short duration of weeping. Then seated on the edge of the examination bed, without further ado the young woman tells her story, a simple type of story that people go through all the time: Lucie wanted to see Paul without Charles-Henri knowing.

Lucie wanted to spend two days in Marseille with Paul, just a quick incognito getaway to see him, there and back on the sly during the weekend, without too much fuss. Meyer, suddenly envious, can picture the scene. But the circumstances complicate her little escapade: first the flaming car then the shaking earth, things that don't go overlooked, risk compromising her scheme's discretion, threaten to push it beyond the realm of the unnoticed.

I can envision the movie clearly, thinks Meyer: *Heaven or Hell, It's All the Same*, a very pricey production, twenty-five weeks of shooting, numerous sets and large crowds of extras required, lots of special effects, Dolby Stereo sound, *starring* Lucie Blanche *as* Mercedes, *featuring* Lou Meyer in the role of the annoying onlooker.

In case you've missed the beginning:

Fearing that Charles-Henri might learn about her trip to Marseille and piece together her liaison with Paul, Lucie sees in Lou Meyer nothing more than a spectator compromising her adventure. She thus keeps her distance from Lou, avoiding any intimacy with him, cutting short all signs of affection, nipping even the smallest desires to see him again in the bud until the scene on rue Cortambert, this last one completely recreated in studio. Afterward we find Lucie, and this is one of the film's best moments, justifying her three days of absence to Charles-Henri: the rapid succession of lies on the balcony, the clamors of a protest below them resounding along the boulevard, and then the line before the sex scene (*"I've picked up the habit"*) are what everyone's talking about. Okay, says Meyer, I think I get it. How about a drink?

They walked away from the infirmary along the tar path

that led silently to the road, weaving between the sunlit palms. Meyer wasn't sure if he should take Lucie's arm, take her by the shoulder or something. Don't worry, he said to her, I won't be indiscreet. At the corner of the road, a little ashen crane, standing in a ditch, grudgingly flew off as they approached.

At the mess hall, one drink later, they outlined the end of *Heaven or Hell, It's All the Same*: Lucie learns of Paul's death in the earthquake. Nice shots, very expressive, of silent torment in the aboveground metro. But life goes on, Lucie goes back to work, breaks up with Charles-Henri, prepares for the space flight. Paul is cried over, soon forgotten, Lucie believes she's protected from her past until she runs back into Lou in the second elevator scene. You know the rest. You're not too mad at me?

No, said Meyer, I've picked up the habit.

27

AND WE'RE OFF AGAIN it seems. At the end of the countdown and with the command for ignition, the boosters' powder is set ablaze. But the spacecraft doesn't take off right away. For a moment it remains fixed to the launch pad, appearing to tip over on its base like a sawed tree; but then, returning to an upright position, it leaves the ground, hesitatingly tears away, not much faster than a moped going uphill. We rise up with the thrust of the propellants and to the technicians' applause.

A small muscle, in the control room, quivers beneath Blondel's cheek. Dakota pisses joyously on the consoles, behind which twenty-five rocket scientists half-heartedly bang their hands together, an underpaid slap, weary from having seen this spectacle a hundred times, even if the blast off's roar causes the ground to shake beneath their feet once again. Outside, frigates, ibises, and violetears flee palm trees bent over by the exhaust gas, the creepers and crawlers in the mangrove scatter in disarray, each one to the best of it abilities, from the anaconda to the crocodile, the sloth to the iguana. This is certainly not the first take off since this group of fauna has settled in near the spaceport, they've surely gotten accustomed to it, it's hardly more bothersome than the siren drill every Thursday at noon.

We're off again. It's exciting, of course, but at first it seems kind of long, nearly ten minutes spent crushed by the pressure and surrounded by the shaking, the rumbling of nozzles and the cranked up sound from the speakers, the nasally orders from the control room given in an urgent tone that heightens your anxiety, squeezed into your custom-fitted bunk like a silver spoon in a case. It's long but it's soon over. We've now injected ourselves into orbit and the silence returns, the pressure diminishes then disappears, we're traveling at last, music of the spheres, through the interstellar cosmic void.

Meyer, on his bunk, undid his helmet's fastener before carefully removing it, freeing his head and making sure that it was possible to breathe, as promised, without difficulty. Then, awkward movement, he dropped his helmet and quickly reached out a hand to catch it—but no, the object was floating in midair right where it'd started. It begins, he said in a low voice. During the ascent, Bégonhès and I had ceaselessly been trickling out a series of numbers and letters, at present we were catching our breath a little, trading a couple short sentences. Here we are, old chap, Bégonhès said. Then, turning toward the others:

— Don't bother getting up right away, he advised, you've got a good two hours before the experiments. Get used to the environment first, try out some simple movements where you already are to practice. You'll see that in reduced gravity you can bang up your face just as easily as anywhere else. Let's go, DeMilo.

Head first and not without grace, guiding ourselves with simple light hand placements, we propelled ourselves horizontally toward the flight deck. From the back of the cabin, Meyer watched our movements, taking note of where our hands went. Didn't seem so hard. Below him, Lucie unbuckled a strap with a series of plastic clicks while Molino, on the mattress above, remained as immobile and silent as death itself. What would we do with his remains, Meyer thought absentmindedly while unfastening himself. Then, trying to leave his bunk without any further delay, Bégonhès's warnings were immediately validated.

Though still managing to make progress, it seemed to him, just like he saw us do it; but even if he thought he was reproducing the movements he'd observed, he quickly realized that nothing was going quite as well as expected. The fact is that you easily bang up your face in this environment, it's just that you bang it up differently. Leaning against the post of his bunk, Meyer takes off too quickly without planning how to restrain himself and slams into the upper bunk—a perpendicular push that immediately sends his body into a spin. Having lost all control, he begins turning over on himself in the middle of the cabin, bangs against the things surrounding him, tears off various accessories from the walls, which then get sent into a chaotic waltz; every movement meant to avoid them complicates Meyer's rotation, who manages, finally, to grab a handle, which he breathlessly clings to; here, you don't only bang up your face, you lose your breath quickly as well.

Hanging on upside down, it seems, his chest followed by his legs floating obliquely above him, Meyer, forcing back waves of nausea, doesn't immediately notice Lucie laughing softly, no doubt with her eyes on him. Goddamn job. I've gotten off to a bad start. He tries to turn himself in her direction while putting on a vague comic saddened smile, but from his position all he can see is, the wrong way round, Molino, not dead at all.

Having carefully stabilized himself, with very delicate movements measured down to the nearest gram, Meyer then tried to move toward the flight deck. But it's still difficult going head first, in a scuba diver pose, it might seem natural but it's not as easy as it looks. He stumbled several more times into the utensils before getting through the passageway and joining us. Before the immense windshield we conversed like two on-duty sentinels, in front of our camera-flanked consoles, Dictaphones and magnetic tapes fastened to the walls with clips, with rubber straps; between our two chairs, within arm's reach, floated a calculator. On my side I'd already stuck up, in the frame of a VU meter, a small hologram of Jacqueline in a bikini; from the end of a straw planted into a container, I sucked up a strawberry liquid while our flight commander chewed on a lime-flavored piece of gum.

Aiming for Bégonhès's chair, Meyer managed to reach mine

without too much difficulty. Tense at the back of the seat, feet wedged into the posts, he glanced out the windshield over my shoulder: blue, white, indefinitely.

Get something to drink, Louis, I said, pointing to my strawberry-flavored container: at the end of my straw a sphere of quivering liquid had begun to take shape, bubblegum pink, the size of a ping-pong ball, with miniature waves rippling through it. As I bent over toward the star tracker, the sphere shuddered and then came off the straw, immediately splitting into two small globes that began to drift obliquely through the cabin toward a bug-eyed Meyer. I caught them just in time and sucked them down in mid-flight with the end of my straw, one after the other. Well, Bégonhès insisted, what'll it be, Louis? Mineral water, soda, fruit juice, coffee, vitamin-enriched milk, whatever you want. Help yourself.

Don't mind if I do, thought Meyer as he looked toward the automatic dispenser less than three meters away, but I'm not sure if I'll make it that far. I'm okay, he said, not right now. He was holding on so hard to the back of my chair that his phalanxes had turned white. Take it easy, I advised him, no use in squeezing like that. I'll get you something. Malted milk?

— Mm, said Meyer with disappointment, isn't there something a little more fortifying?

— Everything with alcohol is rationed, Bégonhès informed him, sorry. It's planned like that. There'll only be one or two occasions to have a drink.

— Fine, said Meyer. In that case, malted milk.

I freed myself from my chair and flew off—I loved this— toward the dispenser while Bégonhès looked over one of the checklists. That's right, he continued, two occasions: the TV relay over Hawaii, the day after tomorrow, and then Molino's birthday the day before we go back.

— Oh really, Meyer said with interest. How old will that make him, Molino?

— Fifty-two, I think, fifty-three. The behaviorists made him a cake.

Releasing the chair for a moment with a sigh, Meyer again lost his equilibrium, pushed backward by his own sigh as if it were a back-up jet engine, barely managing to hold on by a toe clip. I don't know if I'm going to be able to get used to this, he assessed after swearing through tightened lips.

— Of course you will, said Bégonhès, in an hour you'll be completely adjusted. DeMilo will show you. Otherwise, you can put this on if you want.

A shock-absorbing helmet was stored below the cameras, a light bumper head cover made of crossed leather padding, just like what racing cyclists and epileptics wore in the good old days. Meyer was trying to put it on with one hand when I came back from the dispenser, crawling between two layers of air thirty centimeters above the ground, weaving between obstacles, I loved this kind of thing. Drink, I told him, handing him a little parallelepiped made of plasticized cardboard, then I'll show you some exercises. Meyer took off the straw taped to the side of the container and stuck it through the aluminum cap. It's definitely malted milk, he acknowledged. Still just as disgusting. Though the taste isn't exactly the same as on Earth, just like the flavor of things changes depending on whether you consume them on the high seas, up high in the mountains or on the subway.

The exercises that I then offered to show him weren't too complicated. Once he'd learned how to float on his back, I showed him how to turn around without support, how to gather momentum, how to change direction, how to aim his body. How to grab things and carry objects, all of them equally manageable because here, in space, everything weighs nothing: with no more effort than that required for a sponge or a postcard, at the tip of your finger you can lift a bulldozer, fifteen bombers, the Gare de Lyon.

You quickly get a feel for it, without too much trouble you come up with new strategies for moving using traction, using recoil, and soon floating even becomes enjoyable. In twenty minutes Meyer was able to orient himself, to fly directly from one point to another on the flight deck, I let him do a little simulation in the armchair, Bégonhès sent him to get a mango juice. He was coming along. Keep practicing by yourself, I said, and to demonstrate how easy it is I executed a triple somersault above my chair before sitting back down. End of training. 11:33 GMT. Vehicle in transfer orbit. Checklist: final orbit reached in fifteen minutes and nine thousand kilometers; beginning of experiments in eighty minutes. What can I do while waiting, asked Meyer, what is there to do? Can I make myself useful? There's absolutely nothing at the moment, said Bégonhès. You should be able to see the Earth through the porthole, in the back. Go have a look. Get used to it.

28

BUT IT'S CRAZY HOW FAST you get used to things, crazy how right away you want to show off your progress. With a quick hop and with this in mind, Meyer went back to the mid-deck where Lucie, still on her bunk, was arranging brightly colored index cards hanging in suspension around her. Back turned and silent, holding onto a bar with one hand and the mouthpiece of a sick bag with the other, Molino was looking out the window. Over his shoulder, Meyer saw the Earth, currently yellow and blue, a third of it covered with spirals of diluted clouds, sluggish, colloidal streaks over the Southern Hemisphere. I see it, he screamed to the pilots. Can you see Pau? Bégonhès replied.

Viewed from this angle, the Ocean covering three-quarters, the planet seemed abandoned. The light diffracted by the African dusts, at the top left, reddened the sky above the continent. Meyer identified Madagascar at the exact center of the disc: we must've been directly over Antananarivo. You know it's best not to look too much through the window, he said softly, it's not good for you. Oh no, said Molino, why? Radiation, said Meyer, the trapped particles. Causes cancer. Rumors, said the civilian.

They were still admiring their place of birth when Bégonhès, appearing on the closed-circuit screen, announced that it was time to proceed with the experiments. Interfaces and crystals for Meyer, kinetosis and menagerie for Lucie. Meyer turned toward her: the multicolored cards, like hummingbirds in stationary flight, drifted slowly in front of the young woman's eyes.

Shoved up against the backs of their compartments, the other animals were managing the journey as best as they could. The Japanese guinea fowl sat quietly in a corner, crowded together head under wing, and the rats, cataleptic, scarlet eyes and immaculate fur, tails straight out like a pin, looked like hypnotized jewels, ermine brooches decorated with little rubies. Lucie prescribed them twenty-five sesame seeds each and, for the guinea fowl, three earthworms. More than anyone else, the spider was having a rough time, weaving an incoherent web without any concern for symmetry: but just as disoriented as the spider, the midges released by Lucie, flying erratically, were almost immediately captured in it. I can take care of the guinea fowls' worms, Meyer offered, if you think it's kind of disgusting. You underestimate me, she smiled before leaving to go deal with Molino. He watched her move away then tried to focus—okay, what do I do, now, me. That's right. The crystals.

With the civilian tied up to a special support, stuffed with electrodes and sensors and left with something to read, they were able to relax for an hour. Lucie's hair floated around her face in an impeccable blow-dry, a perpetual perm. Meyer spoke of this and that while looking at her, thinking that in zero gravity a bra loses any raison d'être. Look, said Lucie, do you see that? Coming from the flight deck, a little dark brown ball came rolling toward them through the middle of the air. Yeah, sighed Meyer. Then I shot out like a torpedo, darting after the coffee, which I sucked up with the tip of my straw, skimming over the ground and then returning back to my post while whistling *Truth is Marching In*.

But whistling my tune without conviction. I could see that—I know Lucie—there was a risk of something happening between her and Meyer, I could see it from the end of our stay at Kourou. I don't claim to have felt indifferent about it, to have not felt any jealously, of course not, but I let nothing show:

maintaining my smile while continuing to whistle, which is
already a difficult task, I went away as if it was nothing at all.
Showing my feelings would only have worked against me. Let
it be, we'll see what happens. I'm patient. I know how to wait.

We'd just reached our cruising speed and altitude, three hundred kilometers from the ground and thirty thousand kilometers
per hour, conventional circuit for manned flights, an orbital
freeway on which we soon passed and overtook several satellites. A variety of satellites shaped like tom-toms, sea urchins,
chandeliers from 1950 or viruses, turning around on themselves
indefinitely. The brand spanking new ones shined and sparkled
while others were nearing the end of their career; a few were
out of order, electronically dead, some were falling to pieces.
Then there was the usual debris dragging along off-circuit, on
the shoulders, detached parts from a solar generator, sections of
antennas, once even a large glove.

When Bégonhès murmured on the screen that the time had
come to cast off the first of our satellites, I slipped on my spacesuit and headed toward the vessel's stern. The airlock's door
opened like an iris diaphragm and I dove into the cylindrical
tunnel, antechamber between the populated part of the orbiter
and the small area leading to the cargo bay. After unlocking the
external hatch, I settled in at the controls of the remote manipu-
lated arm. Bégonhès, stationed on the aft flight deck, supervised
the task by means of a dual control system. The spy satellite
was there, codename Royco, large as a little Austin, mounted
on a two-stage launcher with visible welding. I started up the
cameras attached to the elbow and wrist of the remote manipulator, then released the opening of the cargo bay. The doors slid
silently open, revealing the cosmos above me, the void where
sound ceases to exist. Gently, I revolved the spy satellite using
the three-clawed hand system, to put it into position for deployment. Steadying myself with the provided handles in the cargo
bay, I approached the satellite, checked its sighting, corrected the

angle by one or two degrees then sent it off with a small push.

Behind the portholes of the mid-deck, Meyer and Lucie watched Royco draw a slow line in the ether, float away from the orbiter toward its point of blast off, from where it would depart for more distant skies. Molino had nodded off in the back of the cabin, floating at an angle in front of the *Get Away Specials*, mouth half-open and eyes shut tight, arms bent lightly in front of him. Meyer touched Lucie's shoulder with the end of his fingers: he fell asleep, he said quietly, what do we do? Should we put him on the bunk? As she whispered to let it be, that he was fine like that, Meyer let his fingers linger on her shoulder, then settled the rest of his hand there—his palm, his thumb—no less gently than one of the remote manipulator's claws. She allowed it. The civilian sleeping, Bégonhès busy on the aft flight deck, myself on an extravehicular outing, they found themselves alone in the vessel, at peace for a moment. I suspected more than ever that something was going to happen. Forcing away the thought, I focused on my task as best as I could.

Cream of onion soup from a tube at dinner, meat prepared wild boar style, rehydrated vegetables, still water. Always critical when it comes to water, Lucie would reproach this one for its slight aftertaste of permanganate. After the tray of pudding, we relaxed a bit with our coffees. Bégonhès told two stories that are funny for astronauts but which there's no point in repeating, which can't be understood unless you practice the trade. Are you okay, Molino? he said, are you holding out all right? I'm fine, said the civilian, swinging his hand in pronation then describing a flu-like lethargy with obstruction of the sinuses and bouts of nausea. Lucie took several notes.

— Classic signs of kinetosis, Bégonhès diagnosed, that's the usual syndrome. It's the absence of horizon that does it.

Everyone goes to sleep afterward in the spacecraft but everyone sleeps poorly, and no more than three or four hours at most. As soon as you close your eyes you feel like you're going to fall, very intense and fleeting dreams flash through your mind, above you the civilian won't stop flopping around on his bunk. Something bothering you, Molino? Meyer asks. I can't fall asleep, the civilian says in a hushed voice. It must be that nap I took. Shouldn't have done that.

He eventually drifted off but upon waking he experienced further difficulties, regurgitating his breakfast just like I was afraid he would. I helped Meyer clean it all up, hunting down the little grayish balls suspended throughout the cabin, sponging the bulkheads spotted with hemispheres of café au lait. Vote Molino. Whom Lucie set up in a calm place, next to a porthole. His face washed, his forehead covered with a moist glove, the elected official watched a gigantic storm above Central America, a dense mass of nimbi illuminated by flashes of lightning coming from below. Then the Atlantic turned a page and the West appeared, the Near and then the Far East, forest fires and monsoons, here and there spurted forth red and yellow spatters from armed conflicts. From a flaming oil field and a restless volcano two lines of smoke rose up, two long stems swaying up to the stratosphere where two black flowers came into bloom. And finally, the unmade-up eye of a cyclone demolishing the Philippines.

29

IN THE TWO DAYS THAT FOLLOWED, everything soon became somewhat repetitive. The animals had calmed down. The rats and the guinea fowl were resocializing, even the jellyfish seemed more relaxed. The spider, getting a grip on himself, had started creating geometry again. Even easier than Royco the spy was the deployment of the Argo satellite. Financed by an association of stockbreeders, Argo would allow the ground location of any European bovine—transmitter collars sending out the cow's name, its temperature and its state of mind. Convenient little one-piece contraption, covered with reflectors and not much bigger than a basketball, with a rather well-aimed lob I flung it off, penalty kick, into the interstellar medium.

Distractions were not in abundance. We glanced out the porthole when we passed, fifteen times per day, over our homes. On the second day of flight one of the guinea fowl laid a spherical egg, which we admired then put in the incubator. The third day, for something to do, I offered to organize a little game of volleyball with the ghost head: no success. And then besides running on the treadmill, pedaling on the stationary bike, or putting on a video, not much to do with our spare time. It's calm, it's incredibly calm, it's not much more complicated or dangerous than a trip to, say, Thonon. No vibration, not a sound. No turbulence in space, no storm or gale, never an air pocket; this can irritate certain constitutions.

Molino, for example, who still hadn't broken his habit of

133

unexpectedly vomiting from time to time, began to provide us with serious attacks of claustrophobia as well: earsplitting outbursts from the convulsive elected official, on the verge of suffocation, willing to do anything for an open door, my soul in exchange for a draft of air, for God's sake lower for God's sake this window. When he became unbearable, Lucie injected him with a little sedative. Two hours per day we had a little peace when Molino, tied onto his experimental base, breathed in a bag of premixed gas. We did a little housekeeping between experiments. Meyer was sure to be close behind the young woman while I was occupied elsewhere.

Fourth day of flight, relay over Hawaii. Blondel had negotiated the live broadcast with several TV stations, it was important for us to be ready. The transmission would begin above Polynesia and last until we were directly over Moscow—which would give us, on the whole, very little time. We swallowed energizing gels an hour in advance, a double ration for the civilian. What exactly are we going to do, Bégonhès inquired, never been very comfortable in front of the cameras. Should we prepare something? Nothing at all, I reassured him, just do what I told you. Act natural, and I'll take care of everything. Molino, try to smile a little bit better than that. On air in six minutes. I know I'm going to be bad, said Bégonhès.

Shortly before we flew over Honolulu, I set up the camera. The others arranged themselves at the back of the mid-deck. I slipped on one of my palm tree print shirts, put on some sunglasses and went to float in the foreground, strumming three minor chords on a ukulele provided by the behaviorists. The others smiled behind me and waved to the sublunary viewers, sucking up small amounts of Planter's Punch through the designated hoses. As you can see, I said to the world, everything's going great. Then without letting go of the ukulele, I executed my triple somersault. Bégonhès and Meyer applauded, I could hear Lucie smiling behind me. Girls always get a kick out of these little stunts, I thought hopefully. Though there's also a risk that they might find them annoying. Let's hope that it doesn't play too much in my disfavor.

And now, I announced, our commander will speak to you. As you can see everything's going great, Bégonhès improvised, beginning to blush. No problems, he expounded, nothing to say. We're having a blast. Very soon after that we were closing in on Russia, official mother of the spatial adventure: donning an ushanka, I swapped my ukulele for a balalaika while the others threw little vodka glasses over their shoulders. Instead of falling and breaking, as is customary, the little glasses continued along a slow horizontal trajectory before bouncing softly off a wall. That's great, said an off-camera voice, finished. Credits. Music of the Spheres. What, already, said Bégonhès, why? I was having a good time. That wasn't so bad after all. Blondel appeared on a screen.

— Very good, he confirmed. Perfect. DeMilo, I owe you one. You were good, Bégonhès, yes, yes you know that you were very, very good. You know that you're sincerely good.

— I thought it was kind of short, said Bégonhès, it seemed short to me. Any news on Cosmo?

— It shouldn't be much further.

Indeed, that very night, after a high-speed chase of three million kilometers and sixty-six revolutions, we saw it at last, spinning around alone in the blackness.

Once the satellite was spotted, Bégonhès ordered the cargo bay to be opened and cut the automatic pilot. While I put on my spacesuit, he manually steered the final approach, positioning the orbiter so that the cargo bay was exactly opposite Cosmo, which we then looked over. The satellite was the size and shape of a bus, weighed twelve tons, and escorted one hundred and fifty autonomous experiments. It seemed to have experienced its own fair share of wear and tear during its extended journey in orbit: several detached parts were floating scattered around it, the spectrometer was in a sorry state and the aluminum panels protecting certain experiment compartments had burst out, rolling in on themselves like the covers of tin cans.

At that moment we were directly above Paris, tearing along side by side with Cosmo at some eight kilometers a second. Fifteen minutes later, while we were flying over the Himalayas, I went through the airlock and propelled myself, the sky wide open above me, toward the space scooter parked at the end of the cargo bay. I undid the anti-theft, mounted it, then full throttle toward the satellite, my gloves turning gently on the handles. The black sky was filled with blue stars, the Earth spun peacefully below me. Alone, crossing the sidereal night, attached to the spacecraft by a wire, through which I could hear Bégonhès talking with base, reporting our actions. Just this once I'd have loved to cut the sound for a moment, but I was already nearing Cosmo.

Taking hold of the satellite by a piece of mooring, I stopped its rotation before towing it within reach of the remote manipulator arm. Then the scooter, with a hairpin turn, brought me back to the arm's controls. Having seized Cosmo, I made it revolve so that, should the operation end in failure, the cameras could film its every nook and cranny. Afterward I stowed the machine in the cargo bay and then went off to bed.

The next morning, Meyer joined me at Cosmo with a brand new spectrometer and some tools; a large paperback notebook with instructions and blueprints floated behind him, connected to his spacesuit with an elastic band. While he carried out the replacement, I checked the angle of the telescope and redid the chambers' protections. It took us the entire day to make the repairs, then a completely refurbished Cosmo was back on its orbit; in the evening, at dinner, Meyer was famished.

We ate then wished Molino a happy birthday. Cake, little presents, a tube of Veuve Clicquot. On the cake, the candles' flames seemed rounder and more solid than on Earth, more difficult to blow out. Happy to be celebrating, happy to be going back the next day, the civilian had relaxed, the medications more than anything else contributing to his good mood. Taking more than his fair share of cake, he sucked likewise on the champagne tube and broke into laughter at the smallest things, then at nothing at all, continuing to laugh all by himself while staring at his knees until Bégonhès, frowning, ordered him to go to bed.

Everyone tucked in, silence throughout the vessel. But no doubt worked up from the day's labor, it was now Meyer who had trouble falling asleep. Glanced below him into the shadows: Lucie didn't seem to be sleeping either, Meyer couldn't tell what she was looking at. Without a noise, measuring his every movement, he slipped out of his support and moved toward the young woman: the orbiter was over Venice for their first embrace, a magnitude 9 on the kissing scale.

Then, in suspension, they spent a long time pressed against each other, floating and spinning lightly above the bunk. Even though Molino was sleeping like a log, drunk off champagne and anxiolytics, they still preferred to go elsewhere. Abandoning their bunk beds, they floated silently toward the flight deck, unoccupied at this hour. Once they'd crossed the passageway, their momentum brought them to the geometric center of the cockpit. Beneath them the consoles conversed in hushed beeps, quiet clicks from the autopilot, Meyer pulled Lucie firmly against himself, running quick fingers over the fasteners of her suit.

As we've already been told, nothing resembles space so much as water. The effect of weightlessness is just about the same. And people imagine, quite often, that it might not be so bad to have sex in the water. It's a common fantasy. All year long, while you're hard at work, you enjoy thinking about how nice it could be. Then as soon as vacation time comes around, the season of oceans and love, you try it out: but you soon realize that, even when you can touch bottom, it's not so easy. And it works likewise in zero gravity. You lack holds, support, resistance, but even so you can manage with enough concentration. The most important strategic fasteners, Meyer located them right away. One after another he began to undo them, right below the lens of an onboard camera that I'd left, inadvertently, running.

The civilian, the next day, seemed to have lost interest in everything. You doing okay, Molino? asked Bégonhès. Maybe the champagne from last night, the elected official theorized. Did I drink much? When are we going back? Bégonhès checked his watch. Nine o'clock, he said, it won't be long now. We launch the last satellite and then that's that.

At 10:00 on the dot we deploy Sismo. At 10:08 I activate the brakeage engines, we slow down immediately; coming out of our orbit, we begin our descent. The service module containing the engines having detached from the spacecraft at 10:33, we're soaring along when we reenter the atmosphere at 10:36. Five minutes of sound and fury ensue, pressure even more intense than at takeoff, radio contact cut, total blackout. Passing through a layer of plasma, the orbiter's fuselage heats up to red then to an orange-tinted yellow. 10:41—the ground is forty kilometers away. 10:42—thirty kilometers. 10:44—ten kilometers.

30

MEYER CAME OUT OF THE MILITARY hospital and proceeded into a crosswalk. In the rearview mirror of an old Fiat, a young woman gave herself a touch-up of blush while waiting for the light to turn green. Besides that, nothing worth noting. The people on the opposite sidewalk came and went, lost in their thoughts, little gelatinous bags of ideas quivering like translucent flowers above their heads, tossing about to the rhythm of their steps.

Back from Guiana after several days of rest and all sorts of medical examinations, Meyer had landed that very morning in Villacoublay. In the afternoon, last check-up, last blood test, then they'd sent him on his way. Beneath the bus stop, waiting for the 91, he rolled up his sleeve to tear off the little bandage from the blood test. Back to universal gravitation: crumpling the confetti of gauze and tape then rolling it into a little ball, Meyer used the end of his thumb to send it toward the foot of the red light, into the gutter, to join the validated bus tickets, the wrappers from cough medicines and appetite suppressants, from chocolate bars.

Afterward the 91 carried him to the gare de Lyon, then the 65 to the gare de l'Est, from where he returned home on foot, passing through rue d'Alsace and rue de l'Aqueduc. As he approached the border of the Morocco sector, he went into an empty minimarket to get himself a pack of beer, where two female clerks were deep in discussion (— Are you doing good,

Véro? — Yeah. — Did you have a nice weekend? — Yeah.) He
then came back up the rue de Tanger, the impasse of Morocco,
then his stairwell. Turning the key in the lock, welcomed by the
sound of a vacuum coming from the bathroom. Beer under his
arm, he crossed his apartment in the direction of the noise without taking off his raincoat. So, he said, how have you been? I'm
pretty tired, Mrs. Alazar responded. Don't exhaust yourself for
nothing, said Meyer, just do the bedroom and then a quick pass
through the living room, seeing as I'm expecting someone. Just a
quick pass. A woman, Mrs. Alazar imagines. Yes, thinks Meyer,
and I'm having a little fit of nerves. Ringing of the telephone.

— Yes, says Meyer, very well, Mom. It all went extremely
well. I'll tell you all about it later.

— You sound a little tense, Maguy Meyer pointed out, you're
talking like someone inside a draft.

— That's because I'm a little nervous, Meyer acknowledges.

While Mrs. Alazar takes care of the bedroom, he dawdles
in the other rooms preparing the field, a task that ends up consisting of nothing more than storing the photo of Victoria on
the radiator cover away in a book. Though he doesn't bother
taking down, in the kitchen, the photo by Cindy Sherman titled
Untitled Film Still #7.

Lucie arrived too late for tea, a little too early for Campari, right
away she settled into his bed and then into his apartment. This
lasts several days, then she brings over some things. This lasts
several weeks, Lucie uses the lack of closet space, impasse of
Morocco, as an excuse to postpone the relocation of her entire
wardrobe. Meyer talks about doing some renovation work. This
goes on for maybe a month. I wait. Every morning, Meyer leaves
for work at Les Mureaux. Before buying another car with the
insurance money, he happily drives the little yellow coupe from
Marseille, which Lucie has decided to keep: the radio's still in its
compartment. In the evening, when he comes back, they have
a drink, Meyer talks about work, Lucie not so much about her

own. Instead, to take an example, Lucie will advise him to get rid of the couch with the big checkers. They eat in the kitchen and on any given night of the week they might end up going to the cinema, on the weekends they go on drives through the suburbs.

Not every weekend: for example, today, a Saturday, after a call from Vuarcheix, Meyer has to leave right after breakfast. Things sound heated and Meyer is afraid he might not make it back for dinner: it's better if Lucie doesn't wait for him this evening, he'll probably be back late. He bends toward her, reading a magazine in the living room, sunken into the couch. He kisses her, she doesn't get up. They exchange wounded looks, dimmed smiles, hot weather but slightly cloudy, then he leaves. He closes the door and Lucie stops reading. She stares someplace in the distance then suddenly gets up, crosses the room toward her handbag, looks for a notebook in the bag then a number in the notebook. She goes back and sits on the couch, sets the telephone on a square in the checkerboard, just beside her, before dialing a number. I pick up immediately.

31

I EVEN PICK UP A LITTLE excitedly. This isn't like me. A short exchange of words is enough to make a rendezvous, at the end of the afternoon, in a bar near the Alma. I hang up, again rather excitedly, it's bad to get so worked up but, quickly, what to wear? Consulted, the mirror suggests keeping on this classy dark red jacket—on the other hand another shirt, maybe, would be more appropriate. But, too nervous to get changed right away, I gnaw away half of a fingernail before shooting a glance toward Titov, pushed up against the back of his room.

I assumed that he was sleeping as usual, but that's not the case: pressed up against the wall, stiff on his back legs, his body fidgets and shakes erratically. I've never seen Titov tremble, I didn't even think he was capable of it, and yet as I come closer I can hear his teeth chattering. Titov, Titov, I say to him softly. Turning halfway around, he quickly glances at me, I see dilated pupils at the center of his bulging eyes. His body is violently shaken, from top to bottom, by a wave that spreads like a snapped sheet, before he turns back toward the wall. Titov, I continue, what's gotten into you? No response. Normally so calm, indolent even, I've never seen him in such a state. Except maybe one time, when Blondel had stopped by with Dakota; Titov couldn't tolerate the rat.

Placing my palm on what passes as his forehead, I check his temperature. Normal. Then, an eye on my watch, grabbing one of his legs whose nails are scratching the wall, I take the creature's pulse, 95, a little fast but nothing to be alarmed about. Fifteen minutes to three, the Rolex points out in passing, five hours to kill before the Alma. I walk round in circles, I'd love to have someone to talk to. So get out of the house, go see someone. Go see Max, for example, that'd take your mind off things. Fine, okay. Before leaving, as a precaution, I lock the door of Titov's room, something I've never done since he's lived here.

In the street, as always, thought bubbles bob about above the pedestrians' skulls. But instead of swaying peacefully, following in step, these little translucent sacks toss and turn about more than usual, as if battered by a breeze. Impossible to find a taxi; I'll go to Max's on foot.

He doesn't seem to be in the best of shape either. From the fact that his beard has grown back a bit since the last time I saw him, I can guess that business isn't going so good. But I know quite well that's not the case, that his backlog is filled into the next century. But he seems preoccupied, distracted, distant, which doesn't happen very often with him. Moreover, and unusually, Max doesn't let me see his studio. Forget it, he tells me, not the right time. Don't go in, it's not very good. Coffee? With pleasure. We stay in the hall, in front of the coffee machine. Silence. Max opens (*Truth Is Marching In*) then closes a cassette player sitting on the percolator.

Through the half-open door of the studio I manage to get a glimpse of a work-in-progress, a big full-length portrait of Kim Jong Il, which doesn't fit so much either, it seems to me, with Max's style. A lot of superimposed uncertainties, several poorly controlled spurts, a number of streaks and hatchings, of fuzzy patches. No sign of the precision—clinical, frontal—that Max usually employs when he undertakes orders for official portraits. I shouldn't drink so much coffee right now, he says, do you see how bad I'm shaking? Silence. Do you want another? Thanks, I say, but no.

The light has changed when I leave the studio, I spend a moment thinking about Meyer. Above people's heads, the thought bubbles shake more and more, threaten to abandon the occiputs. Then as the wind really begins to pick up some of them shake harder and detach, go flying away like a child's balloon, glide then rise sluggishly, disappearing beyond the roofs. The weather's turned. I try, while walking, to come up with a strategy for dinner, nothing comes to mind. I decide to wait it out. Strategies don't pay off, always better to improvise.

I arrive back home, fifteen minutes to five, three hours to kill. Outside, it now begins to rain. I consider getting changed, but first I close the French window. Then I go into the bedroom and walk toward my shirts. I do a quick run through, I take out a handful. Four, five. Normally I do this fast, my choice made immediately. Now, no. From four or five, to nine or ten, then forty shirts, which I can't choose between, impossible to make a decision. So. I look over each one individually, I review its qualities, the faults and its qualities, the qualities and its faults. Difficult, to begin with, to opt for the classic or for the fanciful. This isn't ordinary either. The classic or the fanciful. The basic Brooks Brothers or the multicolored batrachians print. I, who never hesitate, strive desperately to make a choice. I try, I knew, I don't know anymore. Half past five. Titov howls wildly. I go back into the living room, water is streaming down the panes of the French window. Earlier it was clear water, a normal, rather refreshing rain but now it seems murky, rushing toward opacity. From a light ochre, it grows increasingly dark and soon turns, I've never seen this before, magenta then reddish brown. After a moment, you might even say it was blood.

JEAN ECHENOZ is one of France's most respected living novelists. He has won several of France's most prestigious literary awards, including the Prix Goncourt for *I'm Off* and the Prix Médicis for *Cherokee*. He lives in Paris.

JESSE ANDERSON is a literary translator and writer from Olympia, Washington. His fiction and poetry have appeared in various literary journals and online.